Erin Bedford

Also by Erin Bedford

Academy of Witches
Witching on a Star
As You Witch

The Underground Series
Chasing Rabbits
Chasing Cats
Chasing Princes
Chasing Shadows
Chasing Hearts

The Mary Wiles Chronicles
Marked by Hell
Bound by Hell
Deceived by Hell
Tempted by Hell

Starcrossed Dragons
Riding Lightning
Grinding Frost
Swallowing Fire
Pounding Earth

The Celestial War Chronicles
Song of Blood and Fire

Crimson Fold
Until Midnight
Until Dawn
Until Sunset

Curse of the Fairy Tales
Rapunzel Untamed
Rapunzel Unveiled

Her Angels
Heaven's Embrace
Heaven's A Beach

Granting Her Wish
Vampire CEO

Chapter 1

I STARED OUT THE window of my bedroom and sighed. I love winter time. The way that right after Thanksgiving – or even sometimes before – the decorations start popping up. The lights twinkling at me as we drive down the street. The way everything just feels so much happier. Jollier.

Waking up to the smell of sugar cookies and pumpkin spiced everything was like a dream come true. Did that make me a basic bitch? Well, then sign me up for some Uggs and leggings cause I'm all in.

"Maxine." My mom smiled at me as I popped into the kitchen. She stopped stirring the bowl in front of her and came around the table to hug me.

I let her envelop me tightly, my eyes closing as I breathed her in. "Hi, mom, and please, Max? Maxine is an old lady playing Bingo. Whatcha making?" I opened my eyes to sneak a peek at the bowl and saw the spoon still moving all by itself. Sniffing, I pulled back from her. “So, we’re just doing magic out in the open now, are we?”

Mom smiled and moved back to the table, rolling her eyes. “I’ve always done magic. You just never noticed it before.”

“Like what?” I arched a brow.

She took hold of the spoon, mixing the mixture I knew from sight and smell that it was her famous pumpkin spice pancakes. “Little things. Like household chores – dishes, laundry, dusting.” She shrugged a shoulder like it was no big deal.

I pursed my lips and then smacked them together dramatically. “You’re telling me that all this time, I thought you were the dutiful housewife never complaining about housework and you’ve been cheating?” I opened the fridge and grabbed a soda before popping the top and taking a drink.

“Not cheating just ... utilizing good time management.” She looked over her shoulder at me and then winked. “You should see what I can do in the bedroom.”

Liquid acid flew up my nose. I slammed my can down on the counter as I tried to relearn to breathe. There was nothing worse than soda up the nose. Okay, maybe the monthly gut stabbing pains of being a woman trumped it, but it wasn’t far behind it.

“Are you okay?” Mom turned from the bowl long enough to make sure I was still breathing.

Grabbing a hand towel hanging from the stove handle, I wiped my face and nodded. "Physically, yes. Mentally, scarred."

"Pfft." Mom grabbed the towel from my hands and swatted me with it. "Let's be honest. That happened long before this conversation."

What could I say? She was right. Letting it go, I picked up my soda can and moved to the center island where my mom had set up her last stand. "What's all this?" I gestured a hand at the overly large quantity of baked goods and stuffing mix. "Planning on feeding an army?"

Mom rolled her eyes, her mouth no longer smiling, the skin pulled tight as she frowned. "No, worse, your grandparents."

My eyes brightened, and I bounced on my heels. "Grandpa and Mame are coming?" My dad's parents were the coolest of cool when it came to grandparents. We're talking ice cream for breakfast, buying all the latest toys, nothing was too much for their only grandchild. My brows drew together in confusion. "But I thought they were in France for Christmas this year? They promised to send me an éclair."

"I wish." Mom offered me a small smile, and it took me longer than it should have for me to figure out the reason for her displeasure.

"Oh. Your parents are coming." I bobbed my head and swallowed another sip of my soda. I paused for a moment my eyes staring at the fake holly hanging over the kitchen window by the table. "Why?"

"Why what?" Mom continued to stir even though we both knew it was far past done. It was something for her to do because she had nothing else to do and not because she had too.

"Why are they coming? Did you invite them?" I turned around, so my elbows rested on the island, my eyes watching her face intently. Her eyes were the same cerulean blue as mine. I had inherited the same blonde hair from her as well. I often wondered if it was our magical genes that made me take after her rather than my father's Egyptian genes. I'd sometimes wish that I had taken after him. Dark almond-shaped eyes, silky ebony hair, hell at least I wouldn't have to lather on half a bottle of sunscreen when I went to the beach. However, wishing was a bit like magic. You never knew what you would actually end up with.

"No, I didn't invite them. They invited themselves." Mom sighed and sat down her spoon with more force than necessary, making it bounce off the counter and onto the floor. "Crap." She bent down to grab it, her elbow whacking the bowl and sending it to the ground with a thud. "Shit! See, this is what happens when my parents get involved. I get all ..." She waved her hand in the air as she sat the bowl and spoon back on the island. "... frazzled."

"This is my fault." I sighed and fiddled with a package of walnuts. "I'm the one who said I'd sit down and talk to them but then never followed through."

"No, it's not. Don't blame yourself." Mom moved in closer, wrapping an arm around my shoulders. "This is what they do. They slither their way in, sink their claws into you, and never let go."

"Which was why you severed all ties with them in the first place. I should have told them to shove it the moment they showed up at my school demanding me to change everything about me for their high society bullshit."

Mom hugged me tighter to her side and then let go with a sigh of her own. "You didn't know what you were getting into. The only grandparents you've ever know have been great, so why wouldn't another set be?" She grinned at me as she started to spoon the contents of her bowl onto a cookie sheet. "Don't you have plans with Callie today?"

I could pick up on a diversion when I heard one. Mom didn't want to talk about it anymore. Not that I blamed her. Soon, we'd have our problem right in our face, and we couldn't ignore it. Better to hold onto that denial as long as possible.

"Uh yeah, she's picking me up—" A horn blared outside our two-story house, and I grinned. "Right now."

"Subtle, isn't she?" Mom smirked and chuckled.

Laughing with her, I grabbed my purse and then gave her a quick hug before heading for the door. "I'll be back in time for lights!"

Sadly, we weren't looking at a white Christmas here in Atlanta, Georgia. The air cooled enough to need long sleeves but not so much that we could hope for white powder to line the ground. Another thing that I had learned to stop wishing for.

Callie laid on her horn once more and yelled, "Get a move on! We're gonna miss all the last-minute sales!"

I grinned at the brunette revving the engine of her bright cherry red '65 convertible. "You think you could make an any bigger scene? I think my classmates down at the Academy could hear you flagging me down." I climbed into the seat next to her, shoving a pair of sunglasses on my face.

If I was a basic bitch, then Callie was the very definition of diva. Her hair was fluffed to beauty pageant height, her make-up was always on point, and her clothes were those of a fashionista slumming it with the rest of us lowly peasants. Not that she would ever call us any of those things. Callie might look the part of the rich and snobby, something my maternal grandparents would love, but her father was a local mechanic, hence the awesome wheels, while her mother was an outlet boutique owner, hence the fashion-forward clothing.

Today's ensemble included large framed sunglasses that made her look like Audrey Hepburn, a pearl necklace over a black off the shoulder sweater and a pair of skin-tight jeans that I would have ripped in the first five minutes of wearing them. Of course, it was all topped off with three-inch Prada heels from three seasons ago, the only way either of us would ever be able to afford anything that high class. Though, now that I thought about it, my maternal grandparents probably would have been able to afford this season's line.

"What's the point of being this classically beautiful if I don't let the world know I'm here?" Callie flipped her hair over her shoulder with a throaty laugh and revved the engine once more before pulling away from the curb.

"So, what's on the agenda today?" I shifted in my seat so I could pull my hair into a ponytail. Convertibles were great but not so much for the hair. Callie had to have a bottle and a half of hairspray in hers to keep from turning into Frankenstein's bride.

“Oh, I thought we’d do a little shopping, maybe get our toes done, and then ...” She glanced over at me with a mischievous grin.

“Uh, oh. I know that look.”

“What look?” Callie’s grin dropped slightly but was still there as she watched the road.

“That I know you have dirt and I want to hear all about it.” I pointed a finger at her with an accusatory tone. “Well, I’ll have you know that I don’t have anything to tell. So, you’re tough out of luck.”

Callie pouted and slumped in her seat. “You’re no fun.”

“I’m plenty of fun.” I shot back. “I’m just not the ‘kiss and tell every single detail of my love life’ kind of fun. Besides, I’ve been told enough details today to last me a lifetime.” I shuddered as I remembered my mother’s little slip up about her and dad. T.M.I.

“Come on,” Callie whined. “You have four sexy hot wizards totally thirsty for your sweet behind, and you can’t tell me you haven’t done anything with any of them?”

“Of course, I have, but you already know that bit,” I reminded her. I’d already kissed two of the four guys from school, and I almost had kissed a third. The fourth, well, Aidan was an interesting character. I wasn’t quite sure what to think of him. He was gorgeous in a huge muscle man kind of way but was also quiet. I didn’t know much of anything about him besides the fact that my ovaries wanted to have his love child. However, he hadn't said one way or the other if he was interested in me in that way, not like the others had.

"Remind me again who you've kissed?" Callie asked. I knew she remembered but just wanted to live vicariously through me. Apparently, the hotties at Brown weren't near enough to please her royal highness.

"Dale and Paul."

"And Dale's the brother?"

"No," I shook my head, pulling out my phone to find a picture I had not so stalkerly taken when he wasn't looking. "Dale is the redhead who works in the headmaster's office. Paul is the one with the brother."

"Ian, right?"

"Yeah."

Callie let out a girly sigh. "Man, you have all the luck. First, you find out you're a witch and get to go to this really cool school to learn to turn pigs into frogs." Callie paused to stop the car in the parking lot of the mall.

"Why would I want to do that?" I interjected, getting out of my side of the car.

"I don't know, just because? But that's beside the point." She waved a hand at me to hush as she slung her purse over her shoulder. "So, not even counting the fact that you get to do magic, you also have not one, not two, but four guys who want your goodies."

I rolled my eyes and pretend vomited in my mouth. “Can we not talk about my lady parts as if they are something you can get at the store?”

Callie made a face. “Fine, your vagina. Happy?” I nodded and grinned. “Anyway, you have four totally hot wizards just dying to stick their wand in your cauldron.”

I groaned. “Puns, please. No puns.”

Callie ignored me and continued. “However, you haven’t even so much as let one feel you up. I mean, at least you got to cross wands with a couple of them, but if I were in your position, I’d have at least had them whip out their wands so I could measure them against each other.”

“Not going to happen,” I told her, refusing to acknowledge her deliberate use of the word wands for their genitalia. “Besides, after the last guy I let ... into my cauldron, I’m not sure I want anyone going near it.”

“Pfft. That was ages ago.” Callie held the door open for me as we walked into the bustle sounds of the mall. The smell of pretzels and sales wafted through the air, and I already felt the stress of this conversation falling away.

“It might be ages ago to you, but to me, it was still very much just last year. It’s going to take more than a few magic tricks and a hot bod to get over my first love.”

I didn't add that a couple of kisses from Dale and Paul had indeed rocked my world and helped very much get me well on my way to forgetting about my first serious boyfriend and taker of my virginity, Jaron, who had dumped me shortly after for Western College shores. She also didn't need to know that I had been texting Dale the majority of winter break or that Ian had been late night texting me quotes from his favorite poetry ... along with some mouth-watering shirtless pictures of him reading said poetry. Anyone who said the Broomstein brothers didn't know how to woo a girl was so completely mistaken.

"Alright, alright. I'll lay off." Callie held her hands up in surrender. "But the moment you go from playing friends to actual boyfriends, I better be the first one to hear it." She shot me a warning look that I only half took seriously.

"You got it." I fired off a finger gun at her and then looped my arm with her. "Okay, let's get this shopping spree underway. I have some major stress relieving to do."

"You and me both, sister." Callie giggled and skipped us toward the first of many stores to come.

Chapter 2

SHOPPING WITH CALLIE HAD been exhausting but fun. I ended up with some last-minute gifts for my parents and even grabbed one for my maternal grandparents if they actually decided to show up for Christmas dinner.

That was tomorrow though. Tonight was our traditional light viewing and gift giving, both of them being something I always looked forward to.

"Are you ready to go, kiddo?" my dad called up the stairs as I finished doing my nightly stretches. Usually, I would do it right before bed, but tonight, I wanted to get them done before the light viewing. That way I could hurry home to open my gift and go to bed with Christmas jingles in my head.

"I'm coming," I called back as I made my way out of my room and down the stairs. My dad grinned at me as I landed on the bottom step. He had a scarf wrapped around his neck and a horrendous reindeer sweater on, both too warm for the Georgia weather. “What are you wearing? Planning on some freak snowstorm?”

“You never know, this year might be the year we get that blizzard we’ve always been wanting.” Dad wrapped his arm around my shoulders and led me toward the front door.

I scoffed. “Keep wishing, dad. The day we get a blizzard will be the same day that that sweater come back into style.”

Dad dropped his arm from my shoulders and looked down at himself. “What’s wrong with this sweater?”

“Nothing honey,” My mom came around the corner from the kitchen and kissed him on the cheek. “It’s very festive.” When dad wasn’t looking she winked at me. “Ready to go?”

“Yes, let’s go.” I pumped a fist in the air. “I’m ready to drink some hot chocolate and look at some Christmas lights.”

We all trailed out of the house toward the car. Once piled in, my dad turned the radio on to the station playing Christmas music. “Jingle Bells” filled the car, and we all sang along as we drove down the street. Our first stop was to get our hot chocolate through the local Starbucks, then it was onto the richer neighborhoods that always went all out for Christmas decorations.

After we had our hot chocolates in hand, we drove around at a snail’s pace through the neighborhood. A feeling of warmth filled me that had nothing to do with the temperature of the drink in my hand and everything to do with the love I felt of being with my parents.

"Look at that one." My mom pointed out a dancing bear made out of twinkling lights. I smiled and laughed as he hopped from one foot to the other across the owner's lawn.

"What about that one?" I gestured to the next house where a mechanical ballerina turned on her music box the cheerful melody filling the car.

The next house had us all laughing until our sides hurt. This person had a sense of humor and no sense of decency. The Santa Claus projection on their house did a little jig and then proceeded to moon us all, his cartoon butt covering half the house's wall.

"Well, that was fun," my dad confirmed as we left the neighborhood and headed back home. "Did you have fun?"

I nodded and then realized he couldn't see me. "Yeah, it was great."

"Maybe next year you could bring your boyfriend with us?" My mom not-so-sneakily grinned at me.

"Boyfriend?" Dad glanced at me through the rearview mirror. "You found one already?"

"No," I muttered, ducking my head as my face heated. "Well, not really."

"Is that so? You sure looked cozy with that Broomstein boy," my mom insisted as my face burned even more. Damn her for prying out the details from me and damn me for giving in.

"He's not my boyfriend," I insisted, taking a drink of my now-cool hot chocolate. Whatever, it was still chocolate. I'd take it in any form I could get it.

"Then do you have one?" My dad quirked a brow in the mirror as he tried to keep his eyes on the road.

"Not really." I lifted a shoulder and dropped it. "I mean, there are a few that talk to me, and I even like them but nothing official."

"A few!" The car jerked to the side as my dad avoided hitting the curb.

"Geez, watch it, Wesley," my mom smacked him on the arm as he straightened us out. "Don't kill us all, and I don't know how you are surprised. She is our daughter. It only makes sense she'd have more than a few admirers."

Snorting, my dad pulled us into the driveway thankfully with no other potential collisions. "Of course, she would, but I didn't expect her to like them back."

"I'm weighing my options," I muttered as I got out of the car. "It's hard to choose just one."

"Why choose at all?" My mom grinned at me in the dim beam of the garage light.

"Peggy!" my dad gasped, making us laugh.

"Oh, don't act like you didn't play the field before you married me, Mister Archeologist of the year." She sidled up next to him as she batted her eyelashes as he tried to unlock the front door. "You had all kinds of college students and colleagues throwing themselves at you."

"That is beside the point," my dad tried to argue, walking into the living room.

"Then what is?" I asked, flopping down on the couch my amusement at an all-time high. I loved watching my dad get so flustered when he was trying to be fair but also a protective father. I didn't have that many chances to see it so when I did it was quite a spectacle.

"She's my daughter," dad tried to remind us with a serious expression. "Of course, I want her to do whatever she feels is right, but I also don't want her to be taken advantage of."

I couldn't help but lean forward and grin. "What if I'm the one taking advantage of them?"

My dad groaned and shook his head, kneeling by the Christmas tree. "Please don't put images like that in my head." He dug around for a moment and handed me a small package. "Here, I can see when I'm not going to win, so let's change the subject. Happy Christmas Eve."

Grinning from ear to ear, only half of my excitement was from the present the rest of it from hearing him admit defeat. It was the little things in life really that made everything worth it.

I tore open the wrapper and found a box about as big as my hand. I glanced at it briefly and then gave my parents a curious look before popping the top off. Inside, laying in a pillow of cotton material, sat a necklace. It had a silver chain and matching setting for a green and blue oval stone. The center of it sparkled in the light and had a sort of swirling glow coming from the center of the stone.

"What is this?" I lifted the stone necklace from the box and held it up to the light. As it twirled in the air, the center of it glowed even brighter. It had to be magical or at least electronically controlled.

"It's a talisman." My dad moved closer to me, his hand held out. I gave it to him and watched as he unhooked the clasp and stood to put it around my neck. "I found it while we were in Cairo. They're really rare and usually very expensive, but I struck the guy a deal he couldn't refuse."

"I took him to a store I'd visited there before." My mom smiled and rubbed my father's arm. "You should have seen his face when the guy tried to sell him a still-moving chicken foot."

I giggled at the thought and touched the stone as the metal setting pressed against my skin. "What does it do?" I didn't question how he had gotten it, my dad was always coming home from digs with some new artifact or bauble. The fact that he had brought home something of magical origin? Now that was new.

Dad pulled a paper out of his pocket and read off of it in a salesman's voice. "All of your wildest dreams can come true with this limited edition wishing gem. Made of the tears of a fairy and forged by the fire of the Himalayan dragons. All your wishes can be yours if you act now. Limited to ten wishes per user. Must pay an additional fee to recharge. Wishes of minor origin only, it cannot create something out of nothing, and any wishes for death or other bodily harm to a person will be reported directly to the magical council. Use at your own peril." My father snorted. "Well, they sure do take the fun right out of wishing, huh?"

My lips tugged up slightly. Ten wishes, huh? That didn't sound so bad. Though, I wasn't sure what minor origins meant. Maybe I could only wish for things like a good hair day? Or a chocolate milkshake? Wait, would that constitute as something out of nothing? Well, there went my dreams of being a millionaire. Restrictions or not, it may prove to be useful.

"What are you going to wish for first?" My mom leaned over my dad's shoulder and watched me with growing interest. "Maybe for one of those boys to text you back?"

My dad did not look the least bit enthused at my mom's suggestion. I fingered the necklace, my mind rapidly processing all the possibilities and coming up with nothing. There just didn't seem to be anything I wanted right this very second. No magic in the world would ever replace this moment right here with my family.

"I think I'll save it," I finally said, making my mom frown in disappointment and my dad to sag in relief. "You never know when I might need it, especially with you-know-who coming tomorrow. Might need a quick getaway." I grinned and winked at mom, who groaned.

"Ugh, don't remind me." She threw her head back in a dramatic pose before standing to her feet. "And on that note, I need to finish prepping for tomorrow."

"Want some help?" I asked, following her toward the kitchen.

"No, I'm good. Why don't you head to bed? You'll need your energy tomorrow more than me. I'm already the failure child, they still think they have a chance with you."

I wrapped my arm around her waist in a hug. "You might be a failure to them, but you are an enormous success to me."

"Ah thanks, honey," she hugged me back and then gave me a little shove toward the stairs. "Remember that tomorrow when they start in on you."

I laughed and hollered goodnight to dad before heading to my room. Having already done my stretches, I went to the bathroom and got ready for bed. It was a bit earlier than my usual time, but like my mom said, I had plenty waiting for me tomorrow, and I wanted to be well rested for the battle ahead.

As I laid down on my bed, my phone buzzed. When I saw who had texted me, my lips curled up in a secret smile.

Dale: How was your day?

Me: Good. Heading to bed now.

Dale: So soon?

Me: Big day tomorrow. The grandparents are coming.

Dale: Mancaster?

Me: Unfortunately. What about you?

Dale: Jewish. No Christmas for me. My dad didn't get drunk until after nine so already looking like a Hanukkah Miracle.

I giggled to myself. *Sounds fun.*

Dale: I'll talk to you tomorrow?

Me: Definitely :) Spin a dreidel for me.

Dale: There are many things I'd do for you. Night.

Me: Night.

I set my phone down and collapsed on my bed. My cheeks ached from smiling so much. I felt like a corny school girl with a crush. Well,

I guess I was a corny school girl with a crush. Dale was so sweet though grumpy at times, but he always knew what to say to make me blush and squeal, not that I'd do it in front of him. I saved those for behind closed doors.

If I didn't calm down, I'd never get to sleep, I closed my eyes and took deep calming breaths. Gingerbread. Christmas ornaments. Dale's lips on mine. No, no. Bad Max. Think of calming things, not arousing things. But of course, the more I tried not to think of Dale, the more I did.

Ugh. This was going to be a long night.

Chapter 3

THE DAY STARTED OFF on a bad foot. First, I had forgotten to take the necklace off before going to bed and had a dream of myself being choked by my grandmother when I told her to shove her prissy wand up her butt, only to wake up to my own necklace trying to cut off the air to my lungs.

Next was my morning stretches. I tried to get into my zone, to let all my worries fall away, but the more I tried to focus, the more the ball of energy in my mind's eye went haywire. Something was definitely off, and there was nothing I could do about it.

I took an extra-long shower, washing my hair twice because I couldn't remember if I did it the first time, lost in my daydreaming about sexy wizards taking their morning shower. Then as I got out, I slipped on the floor mat and landed on my ass, no doubt leaving a wonderful bruise to show up later today.

"You okay?" my mom's voice called from the other side of the bathroom door. Thankfully, I had the foresight to lock it, or she'd get to see my legs up in the air. Never a position anyone other than a gyno or boyfriend should see you in ever.

"I'm fine," I groaned out, rubbing my backside as I slowly stood up. "Just trying to kill myself today it seems."

"Well, don't die just yet. You'll have plenty of reason to later today, believe me." She chuckled dryly through the door, reminding me of what waited for me today. No wonder I had a dream of my grandmother, my subconscious was trying to warn me to step lightly, and I was heeding that warning. No fighting from this girl today.

"Is there coffee?" I asked before I popped my toothbrush into my mouth. "Please tell me there's coffee."

"And pancakes."

I groaned again, but this time in pleasure. Pancakes. Now that was what I needed to turn this day right around. I finished brushing my teeth and then pulled on the clothes I had sat on the toilet seat, wincing when my pants scrapped against my bruised butt. That was going to sting for a while.

Opening the door, I found my mom waiting for me in my room a pensive look on her face. "Mom?"

She looked up from where she was staring at a photo of her and me I had on my dresser. Her eyes were slightly watery and made me frown.

"Are you okay?" I came over next to her and placed my hand on her shoulder.

"You were so innocent back then," she murmured. The image in her hand was of me at the age of ten, a grin on my face as we played in the fall leaves. It was one of my favorite memories of us. I was thankful to have a picture to remember it by.

"I'm still innocent," I reminded her with a weak smile. "I haven't committed any murders. At least, that I know of." She gave a small laugh and clutched my hand in hers.

"But you also didn't know heartache like you know now." She sighed briefly before sitting the picture back on the dresser. "I wish I could protect you from the dangers of the world, most of all those that come with being a witch."

I wasn't sure where this was all coming from, but I knew I couldn't let her take all the responsibility for my safety on herself. "Don't worry, mom. I can take care of myself. Plus there's nothing you could have done to protect me from getting my heart broken. It's part of growing up."

"I know." Mom turned to hold both of my arms but didn't pull me into a hug. "I just want you to know that no matter what your grandparents say or do, you will always be welcomed in this house. Never think that if you don't please them that I won't love you anymore. I won't ever do to you what they did to me." Her voice broke, and this time, it was my turn to reassure her.

"Of course not, mom. I would never think that." I pulled her close to me and held her tight. Rubbing her back and making shushing noises, my voice came out muffled against her shoulder. "Besides, they haven't done anything but show up and make demands from day one. You didn't raise a doormat."

Laughing as she pulled back, mom wiped her eyes with the back of her hand. "No, I certainly didn't do that."

"Then you have nothing to worry about." I lifted my chin and made a dramatic pose. "I'm a strong, confident woman. No old fuddy-duddy is going to tell me how to live my life."

"That's right." Mom laughed once more and looped her arm with mine. "Come on, let's go before your dad eats all the pancakes."

We walked down the stairs arm-in-arm to the smell of pancakes coming from the kitchen. Christmas music played in the background giving the house a real holiday feeling. My mom and I stopped in the kitchen doorway to watch my dad dance around the kitchen singing under his breath.

He had the handle of a pan in one hand and was flipping pancakes into the air while doing a little jig. When he caught us staring at him, he paused mid-jig and the pancake he had flipped landed on the floor with a splat. Mom and I couldn't hold back our laughter anymore and fell all over ourselves.

"Alright, alright. It's not that funny," dad grumbled as he proceeded to clean up the pancake from the tile floor. Mom was nice enough to take the pan from him and finish up the pancakes while I searched for coffee.

Taking a cup down from the cabinet, I proceeded to fill my cup with two-thirds coffee, and the rest sweetened creamer. Who said you had to like the taste of coffee to benefit from its life-giving force?

"You're not wearing your necklace?" dad asked right after I'd taken my first delicious sip.

My hand went down to my neck and found it bare as I sat down at the kitchen table. "Oh, yeah. I guess I forgot. I wore it to bed last night and almost killed myself mid-dream."

"Oh yeah?" My mom laughed taking a seat at the table with me. She placed a plate of pancakes in the middle of the table which I then quickly began to fill mine with. "What was it? That mean girl at school or a talking panda?"

I rolled my eyes and cut into my pancakes. "You admit to having a fear of pandas one time, just one time, and you are forever known as the panda girl." I shoved a wad of pancakes into my mouth and chewed them viciously. Freaking pandas and their inability to pick a color. Really, who are they fooling? Black bear or polar bear, pick a freaking side.

"So, what was it then?" Dad sat down on the other chair between mom and me, pouring half the bottle of syrup on his plate. Man was looking to get diabetes.

I slowed my chewing down but didn't look up from my plate. They continued to stare at me, so I took even longer by taking a long drink of my coffee before finally spilling the beans. "Grandmother."

Dad didn't get it at first, his face pinching together as he asked, "Why would you dream of Mame?"

My mom, on the other hand, caught on right away. She placed her hand on my dad's and gave him a look that made him quiet right away. "She means my mother, not yours, dear."

"Oh."

"Yeah, oh," I repeated, stabbing my pancakes with my fork. I could feel their eyes on me like they wanted to say something that they had already said before, but I didn't want to hear it. "Look, it's not like I'm afraid of the woman. It's just she's a lot to take in."

Dad snorted. "That she is."

"Wesley!" mom smacked him on the arm though she smiled.

"What? She is. Don't even try to defend her." He pointed his fork in mom's direction. "Remember how she made you cut your hair because Witches Monthly had declared long hair dead?"

"She really did that?" I gaped at mom, not seeing how she would have let my grandmother or anyone tell her how to look.

She pulled her long braid around her neck, stroking it with a secret smile. "Yes, well apparently, short hair meant you were powerful and assertive. Long hair meant you were subservient to males. They didn't want anyone seeing their one and only heir as being below anyone, let alone a potential husband."

"So, did you do it?" I leaned forward, lazily taking a sip of my coffee.

Mom shifted in her seat uncomfortably. "At the time, I hadn't met your father, so I didn't have as much of a backbone."

"Meaning yes," I inputted for her with a grin and then tut-tutted at her. "My mother, the always-be-yourself woman, letting society dictate her own hair length? I am so ashamed."

"I'm sure you are." My mom rolled her eyes, her voice dripping with sarcasm. "In any case, you have nothing to worry about. You don't have to live under her rules or her thumb. You can do whatever you want. No need to worry about an inheritance because you don't have one."

I threw the back of my hand over my forehead and gasped. "Oh, whatever will I do? For shame!"

Chuckled, dad shook his head and picked up his plate. "That's enough of that. Let's do presents, then we can see if we can manage not to burn the turkey this year?" He raised a brow at my mom, who gaped at him, her hand going to her chest in mock offense.

"I'll have you know that was entirely your fault."

"How was it my fault?" dad argued back, taking our plates from the table to the sink with my mom trailing behind him.

"You were supposed to set the timer."

"I did set the timer."

"Oh no, you didn't, or I would have heard it go off."

My dad wrapped his hands around my mom's waist as they continued to argue over whose fault it had been when the turkey burned, and I watched with a warmth in my chest. I'd take their silly arguments any day over any perfect Hallmark movie Christmas. We might not be perfect, but at least we were family, warts and all.

"How about we open up some presents?" my mom clapped her hands together with excitement.

I hopped out of my seat, mouth still full of pancakes. "Don't have to ask me twice."

I rushed into the living room with my parents laughing after me. Settling onto the couch, I waited for my dad to get into position to divvy out presents.

He handed a few to my mom and a couple to himself but the majority of them ended up beside me. My parents had always been good about making Christmas special even if some of the gifts weren't always what I expected.

"Oh wow," I gaped at a shiny blue blouse that changed colors in when I moved it in the light.

"Do you like it?" my mom asked with restrained glee.

"It's really great. The best of all." It wasn't a lie. I'd already torn through all my presents. I received some books about magic that I knew I would devour the moment I had a chance alone, a set of decorative hair clips, and a variety of other things I could use for college and every day life. The blouse was by far the best gift. I could already see myself wearing it on a date with one of the guys.

"I'm so glad you like it." Mom beamed at me as dad sat next to her on her side of the couch. "I was worried it would be too flashy."

"No way, it's perfect." I jumped up and fell into both of their arms hugging them tightly. I couldn't wish for better parents.

We spent the rest of the morning and well into the afternoon mixing, cooking, and just being a family. The time flashed by so fast I had forgotten all about the impending doom coming our way.

Unfortunately, it hadn't forgotten about us.

Our family time got interrupted by the sound of the doorbell. I hold my hand up and stop my parents from leaving. "I'll get it. Probably Callie anyway."

I took another drink of my coffee cup I had just poured for myself as I made my way to the door, I thanked God for whoever invented caffeine. It really was a miracle worker. I could already feel my energy boosting back to full capacity.

Turning the knob, I opened the front door a big smile on my face only to come face to face with my maternal grandparents. And there went my good day.

My grandmother stood on the doorstep with a sour expression her mouth pinched, and her eyes squeezed together tight. She seemed to have a theme about her outfits. The last one was a pastel as well, but at least this was green. It counted as Christmas-y, right?

Grandfather matched her clothing but not so much the expression. From our first meeting, I knew he would be the balm to any burn my grandmother deemed to dish out. He had a hopeful grin with curious eyes, taking everything in as he held a package in his hand, perfectly wrapped in silver paper and a big bow on top.

"Are you going to stand there and stare at us all day, or invite us in?" my grandmother demanded, and I quickly stepped to the side, holding the door for them.

"Sorry, we weren't expecting you so soon," I tried to explain as she made her way into the house like she owned the place.

My grandfather stopped before me to drop a kiss on my cheek and a soft smile. "Don't worry about her. She's always early for everything. If we start on time, then we're late. I have a feeling even when I die, she'll think I should have died sooner."

I frowned at his words but didn't comment. What went on in their relationship was their business. As long as she didn't expect me to hop to it, we'd be fine. Though, the way she was already reorganizing things in the house had me feeling like that was a wish that wouldn't get granted.

"Mother," mom exclaimed, coming out of the kitchen with my dad close behind her. "We weren't expecting you for another hour. What are you doing here?"

My grandmother turned to my mom, and you could just see how her eyes scanned over my mom's rumpled shirt and jeans, the disapproval clear in her eyes. Well, screw you too, Mrs. Fancy Pants. I already decided I didn't like her. No amount of buttering up or gifts would change that. That's my mom, God damn it, and no one would look down on her like my grandmother just did.

"Margaret." The clear indignation in her voice made me step toward them a bit. "I see you grew your hair out."

My mom's hand went to her braid, and a tight-lipped smile covered her lips. "Yes, a few times over the years. You'd know if you'd been here."

"Well." My grandmother smoothed her hands over her skirt as she sat down on the edge of the couch, all prim and proper. "We've been quite busy with our fundraising and charities. Your father has turned into quite the businessman." Her eyes moved to my dad, and I just knew poison would spew out of her mouth. "Are you still playing with the dirt, Walter?"

"Wesley," my mom corrected her and laced her fingers with my dad's. "And he's the top archeologist in his field. We just came back from a dig in Cairo."

"Oh, I see," my grandmother said as if it were the most fascinating thing in the world.

"And your business allows you to up and leave whenever you want, Margaret?"

"Peggy," I corrected her this time, causing her to look my way. "She goes by Peggy, and mom's shop is the best in town. She's the owner, she can do whatever she likes."

"Well, that's nice." Grandmother's words said one thing, but her tone and face said another thing entirely.

Thankfully, my grandfather had the good sense to change the topic. "I'm happy to see we got here before dinner. We brought you something." He held up the silver box for us all to see. "Would you like to open it first?"

I glanced at my parents, not to get their permission but because I didn't want them to think I was unthankful to them. Mom nodded, and I moved toward grandfather, taking a seat beside him on the love seat. "Thank you, you didn't have to do that."

"Oh, nonsense." My grandfather shifted and waved me off. "It's only natural for a grandparent to buy presents for their only grandchild. We need to catch up after all."

His grin was infectious, and I smiled as I pulled at the bow on the top. After the ribbon came undone, I started to slowly pull at the tape holding the paper together, not sure how they would react to me ripping into it. When I realized I was changing myself for them already, I made a show of ripping the paper off with vigor and throwing it in the air.

"That a girl," my grandfather cheered with a laugh while my parents watched from a distance.

A white box sat beneath all the wrapping paper. I lifted the lid of the box with a giddy grin. I loved opening presents, even if it was from a long-lost grandparent who only wanted to buy my affections.

I unfolded the tissue paper inside, and my fingers touched the ridged surface of a silver garment. The ridges came from crystals sewn into the fabric, spreading across the neckline and down into the box. I lifted the item up and out of the box, the bottom of it falling from my hands in a waterfall of silk as the dress brushed the floor.

"Wow," I couldn't help but let out as I stood to admire the dress. "This is really pretty."

"You like it?" my grandfather asked with a hopeful tone.

I smiled down at him and, in the spur of the moment, gave him a hug around the neck. "I love it."

"Good," my grandmother stated. "I wasn't sure what style you would like, but the woman at the shop said it was the height of fashion. I figured you could wear it to your coming out this summer."

“This summer?” I glanced over at her my brows furrowed. “I don’t remember ever agreeing to that.” Suddenly, the dress in my hands wasn’t a beautiful gift but a bribe to get me to do her bidding, just as I knew it would be.

“I know, but one can hope you’ll change your mind?” She smiled at me a knowing gleam in her eyes.

“Even if you don’t, you can wear it to a party or something at school,” my grandfather quickly interjected. “You don’t have to decide now.” He patted my hand as I sat back down beside him.

I placed the dress back in the box and put the lid back on giving them a tight smile. “Thank you, I really appreciate it.” My grandmother opened her mouth, but I spoke before she could. “And I will think about a coming out but not right now. Now ...” I sighed and gave my parents a genuine grin. “Now, I want food. Lots and lots of food.”

“Sounds good.” My dad did a flashy sort of half bow waving his arm toward the dining room. “Right this way to this evenings delights.”

I giggled at him as I led my grandparents to the dining room. I had just finished setting the table a few minutes prior to their arrival. My dad usually sat at the head of the table, so I gestured for them to sit at the other end. The way my grandfather allowed my grandmother sit at the end of the table and took the seat to left said who exactly wore the pants in their house. Not that there was any question.

Mom followed us into the dining room while my dad went to check on the food. We sat awkwardly at the table none of us knowing what to talk about. I fiddled with my water glass glancing between the three of them. What to talk about? Couldn't bring up school because I knew that would lead to an argument. I so wasn't talking about my love life. It didn't leave much to talk about.

"You have a lovely home," my grandfather said with a small smile.

Mom nodded barely smiling back. "Thank you. We enjoy it."

"Yes. Well, it's easy to be comfortable in this kind of place when you don't know what you're missing," my grandmother interjected.

Mom's brows furrowed, and her face started to turn red. The chandelier above the table began to shake. I gave my grandfather a panicked look, but he didn't seem that worried. He didn't know my mom like I did. She may not have shown me her magic before last year but that didn't mean she didn't have her own way of blowing her top. Now that she could let loose I feared for more than hurt feelings. Any minute now and she'd explode.

Ding dong. Saved by the bell!

"I'll get it." I rushed out of my seat and to the door. I shot a 'help me' look to my dad as I passed the kitchen. He only grinned and shook his head.

Opening the door, I didn't give Callie a chance to say anything before pulling her inside. "Good. We need a distraction."

"Uh, okay?" Callie answered allowing me to drag her toward the dining room.

"Look, mom. Callie's here!"

The chandelier stopped shaking as my mom's eyes locked onto Callie. Her face visibly calmed in the presence of my best friend. "Oh, Callie dear. I don't believe you've met my parents."

Callie dipped her head at my grandparents and took. The seat next between my grandmother and me. "Hello. I'm Callie, Max's best and most well-dressed friend."

Everyone but my grandmother laughed.

"I see you haven't quit taking in strays." My grandmother sniffed, dismissing Callie with barely a glance.

Callie's eyes met mine and I could clearly read the 'Is she for real?' in her eyes. I nodded reluctantly and sighed.

"Here we are," my dad came into the dining room with the Turkey placing it in the middle of the room. "Give me a hand would you Callie?"

I started to stand but my grandmother waved me down.

"Nonsense, no need to waste precious energy on servants work when you have magic." She quirked her brow and then waved her arm in an elaborate swoop.

Rattling came from the kitchen and then the door separating it form us came bounding open. Dishes flew through air, pies danced, and the salt and pepper shaker jiggled. I ducked as a plate full of stuffing almost conked me in the head.

"Mother!" my mom snapped, standing up and just barely missed getting hit by the cranberry sauce. "We don't use that kind of magic in our house."

"Why ever not?" she huffed, the dishes coming around to find their homes on the table. "Either you're a witch or you're not. There's not in between." There was an underlying message to her words that I had a feeling was an age-old argument between the two of them.

"For one," mom slapped her hand on the table. "We are in the presence of humans. Do you want Max to think she can just do magic whenever she wants?"

Grandmother didn't answer, her nose was stuck to far in the air it was affecting her hearing.

“Second,” my mom continued. “In this house we believe in doing what we can by hand. We don't want Max to grow up abusing her powers and never learning to do anything herself.”

This time grandmother snorted. “Well, that's not exactly true. If you had your way she would have never learned of them in the first place.”

“Now, dear...” my grandfather placed his hand on top of hers trying his best to soothe her.

“No dear nothing.” She pulled her hand away and picked up her fork. Instead of waiting for my dad to take a seat and cut the turkey the turkey cut itself and a few pieces flew to her plate.

My mom was ready to boil over again, and we hadn’t even gotten through the first course. Dad quickly took his seat and started to divvy up the rest of the food.

“Why don't we dig in before it gets cold?”

Following his example, I piled food onto my plate before shoveling it into my mouth with approving sounds. “This is really great, dad.”

“Quite right. Excellent job.” My grandfather nodded approvingly.

“Right on, Mr. N.” Callie grinned, holding her fork up.

We ate in silence for a few moments the tension in the dining room thicker than the gravy. Eventually, my grandmother decided she had had enough of the quiet.

"Maxine," she addressed me and I snuck a why is me look at Callie before answering.

"Yes?"

"How are you liking Winchester Academy so far?"

Happy she had picked a topic that they couldn't argue about I eagerly said, "It's really great. I mean besides the obvious drama I had last semester."

My grandmother hummed over my answer and then took a drink from her water glass. Sitting it down, she cut at her food. "And how are you holding up with the tuition payments, Wesley?"

My parents visibly stiffened. They exchanged a look before my dad cleared his throat and shifted in his seat. "We're doing just fine."

"Really?" my grandmother's voice went up an octave her brows shooting to her hairline. "Because I have it under good authority that you are currently behind."

"Mother, this is not the kind of thing we should be discussing in front of Max and Callie."

"Why ever not?" my grandmother glanced my way. "I would think Max would like to know that her education is being taken care of."

Feeling embarrassed for not just myself but my parents, I sunk down in my seat. Mom turned to me, her expression soft. “Don't worry, honey. We're taking care of it.”

“Okay,” I nodded my throat thick with emotion. Callie placed her hand on top of mine giving it a squeeze. I smiled weakly at her.

My grandmother didn't seem to notice or care how humiliated she was making my parents feel. Before she could hit them while they were down my grandfather jumped in.

“I think what she's trying to say is that if you are having issues you can come to us. We would be more than happy to help pay for Maxine's tuition.” He offered me a kind smile.

“And what will that cost?” the barely contained rage in my mom's voice was not light. “What part of her life will you wrap your bony controlling fingers around?”

My grandmother didn’t even try to pretend what my mom was saying was outrageous. Her lips pressed together in a thin line and the skin around her eyes pulled at the edges. “I want what every grandparent wants. What you have up until now have refused us.” My mom made a disgusted outraged sound. “Involvement in Maxine's life.”

My dad anticipated my mom's explosion and placed his hand on top of hers. “While we appreciate your offer. I...we...will take care of

Max's tuition. As far as your involvement in Max's life, that is completely up to her."

"That's fair." My grandfather answered, keeping my grandmother from saying anything further. "Please keep us in mind should it come up."

"We will." Dad nodded and then picked up his fork. "Now dig in. There's a pumpkin pie with my name on it."

When everyone went back to their plates Callie leaned over and whispered, "Holy crap on a cracker that was intense."

"You're telling me." And I had a feeling it was only going to get worse.

Chapter 4

NEW YEAR'S CAME SOONER than I expected, and for once, I was dreading it.

"I don't know why you're so long in the face," Callie called over her shoulder as she flipped through the clothes in my closet. "You have four hotties waiting for you back at school. I'm sure you could call up any one of them, and they would rush to be your kiss at midnight."

I tipped my head back from where I laid on my bed to look at her. "I'm not about to text one of them this close to New Year's like some kind of desperate loser. Besides, I might not even get to stay there. Why get attached?" While my parents reassured me that everything was fine, I knew they were lying. Things were not fine, but I didn't know what I could do to fix it.

I stared at the text messages on my phone, longing to do just what Callie said. I'd kept in pretty close contact with Dale and Paul since winter break, but neither of them had mentioned anything about New Year's.

Probably already had plans. I sighed and rolled over to my front, propping my chin on my hands. "Besides, if they were going to ask me, wouldn't you think they'd have done it by now?"

Callie snorted. "You're the hot shit on campus. Maybe they're intimidated by you? You are some kind of magical royalty, aren't you?"

Rolling my eyes, I moved off the bed. "Not really, I mean, my grandparents are famous for something or another, but that doesn't have anything to do with me. Sure, I could use their name to get what I wanted, but I'm not going to do that to the guys I like. That'd just be f'd up."

"*With great power comes great responsibility,*" Callie said in a low and booming voice. "Or at least it worked for Spiderman." She shrugged and went back to invading my closet. She'd already picked her own outfit out, a pair of low riding jeans and a backless blood red top held together by two tiny sets of ties. She had colored her lips a dark red and her eyes a smoky brown, giving her a 'seductress of the night' kind of vibe. I felt bad for any guy she got her claws into tonight. She was going to eat them alive.

"I don't think the web-slinger had to worry about abusing his status to get a date." Sighing once more, I reached over her and grabbed the dress I already knew I was going to wear. I slipped out of my shorts and tank top and pulled the dress over my head. The silky material slid along my skin and settled at mid-thigh. The sparkling yellow dress complimented my skin tone and made me feel like a fairy princess. The straps were thick enough I could wear a bra beneath it, but the material thin enough that if I weren't careful, my underwear lines would show.

"Here." I turned to see Callie holding up a thong by the string. I reached for it, but she pulled it out of my reach with a smirk. "Be careful now, this magical device not only hides unwanted panty lines but, if seen, will attract the opposite sex at mass, sending them into a mouth-foaming frenzy."

Rolling my eyes, I snatched the underwear from her and proceeded to switch out mine. "Haha, very funny. If I were planning on showing anyone them. Which I'm not."

"Not even for Dale?" she teased while fluffing her hair in the mirror.

I paused and thought about it for a second. The redhead had slowly but surely made his way from friend to love interest to sex dream occupant. After the kiss we had shared, I had to say I couldn't really deny the way my body warmed at the thought of him getting his hands on my panties.

"Hey!" Callie lifted up the necklace my dad had given me and turned toward me. "You should wear this tonight."

My lips twisted to one side. "It doesn't really go with my outfit." I reached over and took the necklace from her, staring down into the blue-green stone. "Besides, I don't want to accidentally wish something and rain down magical havoc on the unsuspected mortals."

Callie giggled. "Speaking as one of those unsuspecting mortals, any party of Olivia's could use some livening up."

I couldn't argue with her. Olivia Pecoski went to high school with us and threw a New Year's party every year, and every year it was so dull that most of us were half asleep by the time the clock struck twelve. The only reason we even went was that it was a tradition. It seemed that just because we had all gone our separate ways for college didn't mean that she would change it.

"Enough about me." I sat the necklace back onto my dresser. "What about you? Going stag? What happened to all the hotties you were claiming to be at Brown? Couldn't get one to come home with you huh?"

Callie snorted. "Those guys don't hold a candle to yours. I'm forever ruined by the magical genes of Winchester Academy." She sighed and stared off into nothing.

"You never even stepped foot on campus," I reminded her as I applied my own makeup. "How do you know there's anyone to ruin you for all other guys? Maybe I got them all?" I grinned at her through my mirror above the dresser. I slashed some pale pink lip gloss over my lips and then applied mascara and liner.

"Like you have the monopoly on hot guys?" she quirked a brow at me and then suddenly took the eyeliner pencil from me. "Here, let me." I closed my eyes as she continued to line my eyes. "Just because I haven't been on campus doesn't mean I didn't see the people going in and out of the gates. And let me tell you, there are some fine pieces of work in there. I'm talking orgy worthy specimen." She smacked her lips together as I laughed before pulling back from my face. "There. All done."

I opened my eyes and glanced in the mirror. Happy that she hadn't turned me into a raccoon, I took the pencil from her and put it away. "Alright then, let's get this thing over with."

"Ooo, tingles just went up my spine." Callie shivered and cooed. "You sure know how to put a girl in the mood to party."

I shoved a hand at her back and pushed her toward the door. "Come on, Cinderella. Time to find your prince charming."

Callie scoffed. "Yeah, right. I'm more likely to find a pumpkin than a prince." She dug her heels into the carpet and spun on me, pointing at my feet. "And talking of pumpkins, you better cover yours up unless this is your plan to dissuade the locals with your hairy hobbit feet."

I wiggled my toes with a grin. "Oh right, shoes." I moved toward the closet as I threw over my shoulder, "I'll meet you downstairs. And my feet aren't hairy."

"Whatever you say, Bilbo." She winked and giggled before heading downstairs.

Digging through my closet, I found a pair of sparkly silver heels. I didn't plan on dancing tonight. Olivia's house wasn't really meant for that kind of activity, not that some of the couples wouldn't try. There'd be drinking, food, and talking. Maybe a few childish games like spin the bottle but nothing that would require me to have comfortable shoes, not unless there was a zombie outbreak, but what's the likelihood of that happening on New Year's Eve? I was more worried about my own emotions going out of whack and causing some kind of magical catastrophe, especially since I knew Jaron would be there tonight.

The thought of my ex-boyfriend and breaker of my heart made me clench my hands into fists. He shouldn't affect me like this anymore. It's been almost a year since we broke up.

Besides, I had more than enough guys to keep my attention. Better guys. Sure, they had their own set of problems, but every single one of them was better than Jaron.

Then why did I still have a feeling of desperation at showing up to the party alone? What if Jaron showed up with a date? Would I be the only one there without someone to kiss at midnight? Suddenly, going to this party didn't seem like a good idea.

As I headed for the door, I caught sight of the amulet again. Maybe. My feet started toward it before I could completely form my thought. I picked up the amulet and stared down at it. Chewing on my bottom lip, I agonized over using it. My dad wouldn't have given it to me if he didn't want me to use it, right? And it wasn't like it was a life-changing wish, I just want someone to kiss at midnight, so I don't look like I'm still pinning away after my ex. Which I wasn't. Not. At. All.

Holding the amulet close to my heart, I closed my eyes and muttered a wish. Callie's voice called out, startling me. I dropped the amulet back down and stared at it for a moment before shaking my head with a frown. Heading downstairs, I worried over what I had done.

What was I thinking to make such a silly wish? Now with my luck, instead of worrying about Jaron catching me alone like some loser,

I'd be worried about the magical ramifications of my wish. What was that saying?

Be careful what you wish for, it might just come true. In this case, I hoped the amulet was a dud, and I was just making myself worry for no reason.

"What's wrong?" Callie asked, waiting by the front door. "You look like you're going to vomit."

I forced a smile on my lips and shook my head. "No, I'm fine. Just nervous about seeing everyone after so long."

"Well, don't. You look hot." She licked her finger and hissed as she pretended to burn herself on my skin. "Besides, if someone says anything, you could already turn them into a toad."

"No, she can't." My mom appeared in the kitchen doorway a stern look on her face. "No magic in front of humans. You're lucky that you're Max's best friend, or we might have had to wipe your memories."

Callie's eyes widened, and a look of terror came over her face. "You wouldn't do that, would you, Mrs. N? I wouldn't dare tell anyone about you guys' secret, you know, that right?" She glanced between the two of us, the worry on her face getting worse the longer we remained silent. "Come on, I'm like a daughter to you."

My mom and I exchanged a look before bursting into laughter, causing Callie to stomp her foot and scowl.

"So not cool."

"I'm sorry, Callie. You're just so easy to tease." My mom smoothed a hand over Callie's hand and hugged her close before turning her gaze to me. "I was being serious about the magic though. No magic. Not even to fix your makeup."

I made a face. "Like I would try. I'm still learning here, I'm more likely to liquify myself instead of fixing it."

My mom patted me on the shoulder. "I doubt that, but in any case, I'm happy to know that you have a firm sense of fear for your abilities. It will help you stay out of trouble." She hugged me quickly before pushing us toward the door. "Don't be too loud coming home, your dad has a red-eye flight tomorrow, and you know how cranky he can get."

"Okay, bye. Love you!" I called out as Callie and I headed out the door.

"How sucky is it that your dad has to work on New Year's Day?" Callie climbed into her car as I got in the other side.

I shrugged. "He loves his job. If he didn't, I'm sure he wouldn't do it."

"If you say so." Callie turned the key in the engine but, instead of pulling out onto the street, turned to me. "Are you ready to party?"

"Sure."

"No, that's not going to work for me." Callie shook her head in disappointment. "I need more oomph. Say it like you mean it! Are you ready to party?"

Unable to help myself a grin crept up my face. "I'm ready!"

Callie whooped and bubbled in her seat. "Alright, that's what I want to hear!" Pulling out onto the road, she blared the music as we drove down the street. Our music was soon drowned out by the music pouring out of Olivia's two-story house.

Olivia's house was only a few blocks away, technically close enough to walk but who wanted to walk in heels when you could drive? It made my mom feel better since that meant if I actually did get drunk, which I had no plan on doing, I could walk home and not have to worry about getting into a car wreck. Callie, who I knew would end up plastered, planned on coming home with me and sleeping there, partly because of the distance and partly cause her dad would kill her if she came home drunk. My parents didn't have that same kind of worry. Strange as it was, they trusted me, and I didn't want to break that trust, even if I was in college and technically an adult.

Or so they say.

Right that second, as Olivia's house came into view and the sight of all my old schoolmates pouring into her house, I felt like it was first grade again, and I was the new kid. I sank down into my seat the closer we came, my eyes barely peeking over the edge of Callie's convertible.

"What are you doing?" Callie laughed and smacked me on the arm. "You're not going to have any fun like that. Let's go." She reached over me and opened the door, shoving me out before I could protest. I had the good sense to grab the door handle before I faceplanted into the grass in front of everyone.

"Why are you my best friend again?" I grumbled as she came around and helped me stand.

"Sorry," she half-laughed. "I didn't mean to manhandle you so much. I just don't want you to let your fear of seeing Jaron ruin the party for you."

Brushing myself off, I glanced around discreetly hoping no one had seen me face plant. "I'm not worried about seeing Jaron."

Callie snorted. "You can face the mega-sonic bitch of all mean girls, but you can't face your ex-boyfriend?" Not waiting for me to grow a pair, Callie started toward the front door, smiling and greeting everyone she saw.

"That was different," I claimed, catching up to her at the door. Olivia stood at the entry grinning from ear to ear. Her dark hair was twisted up into some kind of Chinese updo I could never replicate, no matter how hard I'd tried. She wore bright green eyeshadow that stood out against her doll-like features. Olivia had an intense need to make herself look more adult than she actually was. She was perpetually placed in the Lolita category, and she had to compensate by dressing more adult. Well, in her case, adult meant provocative. Her small chest was pushed up to her chin, and I feared I'd be getting an eye full of her butt if she ever bent over even the slightest.

"Hey, Olivia!" Callie squealed and hugged her close before pulling back to look her over. "I love your dress. Another one from your cousin over in Tokyo?"

Olivia nodded, her eyes darting to me then back to Callie. The look she gave me was strange, hesitant. Olivia and I didn't have any issue with each other, not that we ran in the same circles or had anything in common, so I brushed off her peculiar behavior. "Yes! I just got it for Christmas. It's so hot, isn't it?" She struck a sexy pose which only made her look more like a child playing dress up, but I didn't say anything. I knew when to keep my mouth shut.

"It's really great." Callie grinned, genuinely pleased to be there. She turned to me and grabbed my hand. "Come on, Max. Let's get something to drink. Talk to you later, Ol!"

I let Callie drag me through Olivia's house, the music so loud I feared the decorative plates on the wall might fall off and break at any moment. We had arrived about the time everyone else had so the house wasn't quite filled to capacity. Thankfully, that made it so we could get to the kitchen and to where the drinks were pretty easily.

"Here," Callie handed me a beer, and I grimaced. I put it back and grabbed a soda. "Oh, come on, you have permission to drink and you still won't?" she chastised me as she chugged down her own beer.

I eyed her as she grabbed a second can. "I think you are drinking plenty for both of us. Besides, I'm still not used to ..." I lowered my voice looking for eavesdroppers. "... my powers. I don't want to chance blowing up the whole house because I got drunk."

"Ah!" Callie pointed a finger at me. "Good idea. Alcohol bad. In fact," - she set her beer down and grabbed a soda instead, - "I will join you in your sobriety and even run interference if you know who shows up."

I smiled softly at her. "You don't have to do that. I don't want to ruin your fun because of my handicap."

"If you're sure." Callie quickly picked her beer back up with a grin and wink. "I plan on getting shit faced and make out with someone I won't remember in the morning."

Laughing at her, I took a drink of my soda and scanned the kitchen. There were a few I recognized from high school, but it seemed a lot of them were people I didn't know. Olivia's parents were nowhere to be seen which was normal. They were usually out on business and left her home alone. It was the only way she was able to have such big parties without getting into trouble.

"Think the cops will break it up this year?" I asked as Callie led us through the kitchen and to the living room where some people had begun to dance around. At least two times before, we had the cops called on us, but Olivia's dad was some big shot lawyer, and Olivia never ended up in trouble or anything for the underage drinking going on. That'd have never gone over in my family. Well, now that I thought about it, my mom could have magicked away their memories. It also made me wonder if she had ever altered mine.

"God, I hope not." Callie moved her body to the beat of the music, wiggling my arms and trying to convince me into dancing. I laughed and shook my head before giving in by shimming a bit. My shimming changed to a full-out body sway that made me regret my shoe decision.

I laughed and danced with Callie letting my mind get off of the reason I dreaded coming. The party was in full swing now and getting more crowded by the second. Not wanting to get trampled, I inched away from the dance floor. I motioned to Callie that I was getting a drink before pushing my way through the crowd. We only had a few minutes until midnight, and I so didn't want to be near Callie when she found her victim for the night.

Someone called my name, and I turned to say hi. My foot caught on someone else's, and I tripped. My hands grabbed the first thing I could latch onto which ended up being a very familiar pair of shoulders. Straightening myself, I released the shoulders and tried to make a run for it, but it was too late. I'd been seen.

"Max?" Jaron's voice made my shoulders hunch up around my ears, and I forced myself to relax as I turned around.

"Jaron? Hi." I hoped my smile wasn't as forced as my voice sounded.

"I didn't think you were going to come." I couldn't tell if he was disappointed or surprised. Not that it mattered. It didn't.

"Uh, yeah. Callie made me." I lifted a shoulder as if it answered everything.

"Well, I'm glad you did." Jaron smiled at me, his dark eyes glazed over already from the alcohol. He looked good even after all this time. His strong nose down to his pouty lips covered in ... was that lipstick?

As I leaned in to get a closer look, a head popped out around Jaron. "Hey, Max," Olivia said tightly, her lipstick slightly smeared on her face, matching the same shade on Jaron's lips. Ah, it made sense now. The strange look at the front door was because she was with Jaron now.

"Hi." I gave her a nod and then gestured my head toward the kitchen. "I'm just going to go get a drink."

"Wait, I—" Jaron started to say, but Olivia spoke over him.

"Okay, see you later."

I didn't wait to see if Jaron would try to talk to me but pushed my way toward the kitchen. I could feel the magic in me making my skin hum. I didn't know why I was so worked up. Of course, Jaron would move on. I had too, hadn't I? Yes, of course, I have. It was just hard to see your first love with someone else. That was it. I was lonely and vulnerable without a date. It was only natural I would feel frazzled.

Instead of staying in the kitchen, I pushed my way to the patio in the back where there were fewer people. A chill came over me, and I realized that, even in Georgia, skimpy dresses in the dead of winter were not a good idea. I was contemplating going back inside or risking freezing to death when I remembered I was a witch now.

There had to be a spell to warm me up. However, what that spell was I had no idea. I could attempt one, but then again, my mom had said no magic. Did I really want to take the chance of blowing myself or someone else up because I was too chicken to face my ex and his new girlfriend?

I started to scour my brain for something I had learned at school to take the bit of the cold off, but I was coming up blank. I had just about given up and decided to brave the crowd once more when a hand touched my bare shoulder, and a warmth came over me.

Glancing down at the hand, I followed it to a smiling Dale. "You looked cold."

"What are you doing here?" I stepped closer to him, unable to believe my eyes. For a second, I thought my wish had actually come true.

Dale brushed his reddish-brown hair out of his face as it fell over his glasses and he shrugged. "Callie text me."

I didn't doubt that for one second. The sneaky woman no doubt found his number in my phone at some point and did the deed for me. I'd have to kiss and smack that girl later.

"Well, I'm glad she did." I ducked my head, feeling slightly shy now that he was in front of me. We had spent weeks messaging each other, but in real life, it was so much different, and my body reacted in such a way.

"So, why are you out here risking frostbite rather than having fun with your friends?" Dale leaned against the railing of the patio. He wasn't dressed in his usual button-down shirt and slack combination he wore to school. The t-shirt he wore stretched across his chest, showing me that he had muscle underneath he had been hiding from everyone. The difference was intriguing and just downright arousing.

Chewing on my lower lip as I tried to get a hold of my raging libido, I glanced toward the sliding glass door. "I ran into someone I didn't want to talk to."

"Your ex?"

My eyes shot over to his raised eyebrows. "How'd you know that?"

Dale lifted a shoulder. "You've mentioned him in passing before, I just assumed that'd be it." I nodded in response, and we grew quiet. After a moment or two, Dale asked, "Do you still love him?"

"What?" I gaped. "No, nothing like that. I mean, he was my first ... love but that doesn't mean I care anything at all about him now." Even I knew I didn't sound convincing. Sighing, I leaned against Dale's side. "It's not that I love him. It's just ... he's a reminder."

"I get it."

"You do?" I lifted my head to look at him.

“Yes, believe it or not, I have been in love before,” he said dryly, his lips twisting into a frown.

“I can believe it.” I had no doubt about it. Dale was dreamy in that intellectual kind of way. The glasses, the attitude, the shaggy hair, and that hidden hot bod? It was any girl’s wet dream when you put all together. Not that I was going to tell him that. I had my dignity after all.

“You’d be the first.” Dale sighed and shook his head. “I’m not exactly a catch back at school. I don't work in the administration office because I want to. If not for my work study I wouldn’t be going to college at all.”

“I feel ya there.”

Dale looked at me like I’d grown a second head. “What do you know about it? You have a rich family. You only have to worry about what pair of shoes to buy. And then end up buying all of them"

I snorted. “I know its hard to believe but I don’t have much of anything to do with my grandparents. They are the ones who are rich, not me.”

“Still, at least you have more than just your personality to get you by.”

I cocked my head to the side. “Why? Because you’re not from some famous wizarding family? Believe me, it’s not all it’s cracked up to be.” I thought back to my grandparents and all the expectations they had for me. I'd rather have been someone like Dale. Things would have been so much easier.

Dale smiled sadly and brushed my hair behind my ear, his fingers lingering on my skin. "You only say that because you just joined our world. If you'd have grown up in it, you'd be just as stuck on status as the rest of them."

I frowned at him. "I'd like to think I wouldn't be, but I can't say what kind of person I'd have been. All I know is the kind I am now." I grasped the hand on my face with my own. "And right now ... right now, I know that you could be a human or the lowest of wizards and it wouldn't keep me from wanting to kiss you any less."

Smiling that masculine kind of knowing smile, Dale slid his other hand around my waist and drew me closer. His mouth descended on mine, and everything fell away. The warmth inside of me from his spell was replaced by the need for him and the touch and taste of him. I let out a moan as his tongue brushed against my lips, and I opened up to him.

Releasing his hand, I wrapped both arms around his neck, my fingers tangling in his hair like I had wanted to do since day one. He cupped the back of my thighs and lifted me onto the banister, placing himself between my legs. I'd have been worried about my dress sliding up, but his body would hide anything from being seen by onlookers.

Somewhere in the distance, I could hear shouting of some kind, but I didn't care enough to come up from the consuming feeling of Dale's mouth on mine. As close as we were, I wanted more of him. I had told Callie that I hadn't planned on letting anyone see my thong that night, but Dale had lit something inside of me that made me want his hands on more than just my underwear.

A booming sound followed by another and another, startling me from Dale's lips. We both looked up and saw the dark sky filled with multicolored sparks of light. Fireworks.

I could see over Dale's shoulder that the people inside were partying harder than ever, many of them making out with their dates or whoever was closest. We'd missed the countdown, but with the guy in front of me making my whole-body tingle, I couldn't bring myself to really care.

"Happy New Year, Max." Dale grinned down at me before brushing his lips against mine once more.

"Happy New Year, Dale."

Chapter 5

AFTER NEW YEAR'S, SCHOOL couldn't come any faster. Unfortunately, I did not get the chance to show anyone but my passed-out best friend my underwear because Dale had to leave right after the fireworks. However, now that school started today, I hoped to remedy that.

"Max!" Trina squealed, jumping up from the floor and a pile of things to hug me the moment I entered our room. "How was your break? Tell me everything!"

I hugged her back and giggled before throwing my bag onto my bed. "It was okay. The same as usual except now my mom does magic openly in front of me. Oh, and my grandparents came for Christmas."

Trina made a face. "Ew, I bet that was fun."

Unzipping my bag, I laughed bitterly. "Oh, you know it was. They got into a fight not even five minutes after they got there."

"Still trying to make you do a coming out thing?" Trina asked, combing a pick through her hair. Over the break, she had streaked her usual ebony afro purple and teal, it looked cool and matched the outfit she had on perfectly. It always did though. How did I end up with such fashion-forward friends when I was lucky to match my socks on any given day?

Sighing, I sat on the edge of my bed. "Yeah, they got me this really pretty dress and then got into the whole not-so-subtle 'you could wear it for your coming out' thing while also trying to take over my life by offering to pay my tuition. Hence the fighting."

"Better than my house. We have fighting non-stop, but with that many of us in one house, it's kind of expected." She grinned and sat on the floor, crossing her legs as she went back to organizing her things.

"I bet it's fun, having that many siblings."

"Pfft. No. I mean, yeah, I guess, if you like sharing all your things and getting hand me downs. But then there's the whole bonding thing. You're never lonely cause there's always someone to talk to and get into trouble with." Trina grinned from ear to ear as she talked about her family. I could tell she really loved them.

"Well, the closest thing I have to a sibling is Callie." I slid down to the ground to sit across from her. "She's usually the one getting me into trouble."

"She seems the type." Trina giggled. "Did she go back to Brown already?"

I nodded. "Yeah, but she's coming back during Spring Break. I hope you'll get to hang out with us this time."

"Oh, for sure." Trina shook her head up and down. "I'd much rather go to a party than watch my parents play charades until midnight." She sighed. "One of these days, I swear I'm going to get my kiss at midnight."

Her talks of New Year's brought back my own memories. Now that I was back at school, Dale would be here. I itched to message him and ask him to meet up, but I didn't want to seem like a bad friend who makes their whole life about the guy she liked ... or guys in my case.

"What's with that face?"

I blinked and stared at her knowing look. "What face?" I touched my cheek thinking I could somehow change whatever it was she saw.

Trina moved to her knees and poked my cheek. "That 'I got laid and can't stop grinning about it' kind of face."

My skin heated and I shook my head. "I didn't get laid."

"But ...?" Trina prompted, and I wrapped my arms around my knees, drawing them up to my chest, grinning despite myself.

I started to explain about New Year's, but a knock on our open bedroom door interrupted us. Ian leaned against the door frame looking as yummy as ever. The kind of shirt Dale had worn at the party was the kind I was used to seeing Ian in. It clung to his pecs and made it impossible not to notice how ripped he was. Tight black jeans hugged his hips and sat over the biker boots he always wore. I swore if he didn't end up having a motorcycle, I would swallow my own tongue.

"Am I interrupting?" Ian smirked, raising one beautifully sculpted brow, his green eyes swirling with amusement.

"No, no." Trina jumped to her feet, her eyes darting between the two of us. "I'm just going to go get a snack. You want anything?" I shook my head, and she beelined it for the door. As she squeezed by Ian, she made an obscene gesture of what she thought I should do with him while she was gone that made my face burn.

When she was gone, silence filled the room, and I shifted on the floor. Ian, ever the one to make a space seem like his own, meandered into the room, his eyes taking everything in.

"How was your holiday?" I asked him out of the blue, not sure what else to talk about. He was hot, but we didn't know that much about each other, something I should probably be working on to fix and not just thinking with my girl bits.

Ian glanced over his shoulder from where he was looking at Trina's collection of hair bows. "You really want to ask me about my vacation?"

I lifted a shoulder. "I don't know. You don't really talk about yourself besides to tell me how fascinating and hot you are. Or to complain about your brother."

The mention of his brother made him frown slightly. "Okay, so ..." He sat down on Trina's bed and leaned forward on his knees, his eyes intensely focused on me. "What do you want to know?"

Putting me on the spot the way he was, I found myself scrambling for something to ask. "How about your major? You're doing the dark arts, right? Like blood magic?"

Ian's face seemed to close off, his eyes darkening at my topic of choice. "Yes, I am studying the dark arts."

Seeing he wasn't going to give me anything more on it, I tried something else. "What did you do for break? Did you and Paul spend time together with your parents?"

"No, our parents were in Aspen. Paul stayed at school for some teacher's pet convention," he muttered, clear resentment filling his words. I wondered what had happened since our last conversation. They had seemed so into getting their relationship back on track, but now it seemed like they were backsliding.

"Then what did you do?" I found myself inching closer to where he sat, not liking the sad and lonely look on his face.

Running a hand through his dark hair, the corner of Ian's lip curled up. "I read and thought about you."

My eyes widened at what he was clearly trying to instigate, but I focused on the other part. Get to know him, not his soul-consuming eyes, or the way his tongue darted out to wet his lips. Come on now, Max. Get in the game.

"Reading, huh? You read a lot." I cleared my throat and looked away from him.

"Sometimes. Mostly research for school but sometimes poetry. I particularly enjoy Edgar Allen Poe."

"So, the dark stuff." I smiled, palming my legs to keep my hands from sweating. "I'm sensing a theme here."

All of a sudden, Ian slipped off the bed and knelt close to me. The heat of his breath hot against my skin. "Beauty of whatever kind, in its supreme development, invariably excites the sensitive soul to tears." Ian's words brushed against my lips as he leaned in my eyelashes fluttering with each breath.

“Who said that?” I murmured curious but not so much that I paid much attention to his answer.

“Poe,” Ian told me, his hand curling along my jawline, his thumb tracing my lower lip. “Do you like it? Is it too dark?”

I shook my head slightly, blinking up to meet his gaze. “It’s pretty. I didn’t know he was such a romantic.”

Ian chuckled, it rumbled through his chest and into my legs where he pressed against. “He was just a man like anyone else. Nothing dark or dangerous about him ... or me.”

It was my turn to laugh, bringing our mouths to barely touch each other. “I wouldn’t say that.”

“You think I’m dangerous?”

Smiling, I grabbed the front of his shirt in my fist. “Hazardous.” Pulling him toward me, our lips finally converged into one. All the teasing had been too much for me, it took much of my strength not to straddle him right there with the door open and everything. Trina would have been so proud. Callie too. The hussies. Though at the rate I was going, I was well on my way to becoming an exhibitionist. With that thought, I limited myself to a few passionate moments of lips locked before releasing Ian to breathe.

"Well, well, well," the voice of Satan's mistress herself snickered. "Look what we have here."

Looking toward the door, I scowled at Sabrina Craftsman, witch bitch extraordinaire. "What do you want, Sabrina? Lose your talking cat?"

"Cats give me hives, not that you care." Sabrina sniffed before she gave me a nasty grin, waving her phone in the air. "However, I'm sure your boyfriend Dale and the rest of the school would love to know you are locking lips with black sheep of the Broomstein family not even after being thirty minutes on campus." She tapped her face with her phone pretending to be in thought. "Or is it Paul? I just can't seem to keep up with your love life."

Gritting my teeth, my fingers began to crackle with magic, and I longed to lash out at her. Ian grasped my hand with his, giving me a warning look. He was right, that's what she wanted. Taking a deep breath, I let it out with an exhausted sigh.

"Go ahead, Sabrina." I stood up from the floor, crossing my arms over my chest. "Send it to everyone you know, I'm not ashamed. I like Ian. So, yeah, I kissed him. And you know what," - I pointed a finger at her, placing my hand on my other hip - "I also like Paul and Dale, and there's nothing you can do to make me feel bad about it. Just because your capacity to love is limited to one person doesn't mean mine has to be."

Sabrina leaned back as if I had hit her, her mouth gaped open in shock. "Wow, I never expected you to be so brazen about your promiscuity." She smirked and flipped her long blond hair over her shoulder. "You might think you're top shit right now, but once this gets out, you'll be back licking the ground I walk on. Right where you and your human-loving mom belong."

I stepped toward her, but Ian's hand on my arm stopped me. I didn't even notice he had stood up until now. He distracted me long enough for Sabrina to slip down the hall well on her way to tell the world of how unworthy I was of my position.

"Why'd you stop me?" I glared at Ian. "I could have taken her."

Ian rubbed the back of his head, a frown marring his face. "Yeah, and get in trouble for attacking a student unprovoked. Last time Sabrina attacked you first, but if you attack her for just being a bitch." He shook his head, his hands opening up to either side. "I'm not sure you want to go using your family name to get out of that one. You might want to save that for when you really have to use it."

I realized he was right. I didn't want to be calling in any favors to my grandparents, especially not for something as petty as burning all the skin off of Sabrina's smug face. I had to save those kinds of favors for when I was in dire need, which sadly looked like it might end up being sooner rather than later.

"So ..." Ian drew my attention back to him, a salacious expression on his face. "You like me, huh?"

I snorted. "Of course, that's the part you lock onto, not that I like your brother and Dale too."

Ian shrugged. "Hey, I'm just happy to be included. If you want to build yourself a harem of wizards or even witches," - he wagged his eyebrows suggestively, making me giggle - "I'm game, as long as I get ample time with you as well."

"Really?" I cocked a brow. "You're not jealous or wanting to stake some kind of alpha male claim on me?"

Sliding his hands around my waist to draw me up against his front, I could feel exactly how happy he was to be there, pressed hard against my stomach. "I fought my whole life to be seen by someone the way you look at me. When I'm with you, I don't feel like someone you settled for, like you'd rather have my brother."

"But I like your brother too," I reminded him, wondering if that would be a deal breaker for him.

“The operative word is ‘too.’ Not more or instead of. I’m okay with ‘too.’” He stroked the side of my face and then dipped down to press his lips to mine once more.

“What’d I miss?” Trina’s breathless voice interrupted. I turned to her standing in the doorway with her arms full of snacks. The girl did not know the word moderation.

Gesturing her to come in, I drew Ian over to sit on my bed. “Let me catch you up.”

Chapter 6

"SO, I WAS THINKING about what you said happened with your grandparents," Trina said the next morning while we sat on our room.

"Oh yeah?"

"Yeah, you should do a booth at the spring fair." She took a large bite out of her muffin and crossed her legs on her bed.

"Spring Fair?"

"You know, the fair. Every year, a bunch of students sign up to make a booth to compete against each other. The booth has to have something to do with your major, and you have to write an essay too, stating why you should win but the winner gets next year's tuition paid in full." Trina waved a hand in the air as if she hadn't just told me something important.

"That would be perfect!" I bounced in my seat thinking of how the fair would take care of all of my problems. "So, what do I do for my major?"

Trina let out a hard breath. “Man, they really don’t tell you guys crap.” When I just stared at her, she threw her hands up. “Okay, so I guess it is up to me to be the savior of all human-raised witches.” She smacked her thighs with her hands. “So, unfortunately for you, you didn’t have all of elementary and high school to figure out what you wanted to do with your life.”

“Yeah, I did,” I interrupted her. “However, I think my fourth-grade aspirations to be an astronaut are kind of out of the question.”

“What’d you want to do at Brown?”

I laughed through my nose and grinned. “Political Science.”

“Okay, cool.” Trina gestured to me with her hands, spilling muffin crumbs over the floor. “So, you can still do that here. Just it would be magical politics.” I groaned before she even finished the sentence. “It’s not that bad. You’ve already got some great connections. You just need to make sure your classes line up with it and think of a platform. What are you taking this year?”

I reached into my bag and pulled out my schedule. When I got my schedule for this semester, I had only glanced at it, not really seeing what was in store for me. Now that I had to actually know where I was going, I took another hard look at it.

On Mondays, Wednesdays, and Fridays, I had Etiquette of Magic first. If someone had asked me what kind of classes I thought I'd have to take before knowing I was a witch, I'd have rattled off something like about psychics and palm reading, maybe even reading the stars. Etiquette, however, would not have been anywhere on that list. Based on the way the hierarchy system was set up with the so-called privileged students versus the lower bloods, I shouldn't have been surprised that I'd have to learn some kind of etiquette. Unfortunately, I don't think that this class had anything to do with place settings and covering your mouth when you coughed.

"Ick," Trina said over my shoulder through a mouth full of muffin. "It's like they want you to crawl back into bed and die."

I wrinkled my nose at her. "That bad, huh?"

"Etiquette of Magic?" Trina snatched my schedule from my hands just shy of giving me a paper cut. "I took that in, like, grade school. It's the kind that even the most astute student wanted to gouge their eyeballs out with a dull fork. Though, you'll definitely need it for your major."

"What about my other ones? Have you taken any of those yet?" I finished gathering up my books as she scanned over the list. Last semester hadn't been that bad save for the time I almost blew up the whole lab in Potions.

I could only cross my toes that this semester would go well too.

Trina hummed and played with the strap of her bright yellow tank top. "Most of these are pretty basic. Ooo!" she shouted suddenly pointing a finger at the paper. "I have Potions 2 with you. Ugh," she added with a grimace. "And P.E."

"P.E.?" my brow furrowed in confusion. I hoped I had heard her wrong. P.E. had to stand for something magical right? *Philosophies of Elementals* or something equally as obscure? There's no way in this green earth that it meant what I thought it meant. Could it?

"I can feel my blood pumping already. I can't wait to get my body moving. I'm going to kill some calories." Trina moved her arms and hiked up her legs up like she was marching in place. There was a fire in her eyes that I'd never seen before.

"Please tell me this isn't what I think it is." I buried my head in my hands and groaned. "I thought I was done with all the running and the pushups when I graduated high school?"

"You don't like P.E.?" Trina looked at me like I had grown a second head. Apparently, physical fitness was not something we had in common.

"No way."

"Maybe you can get your new boyfriend to get you out of it?" Trina raised a brow and grinned at me.

That actually wasn't a bad idea. Dale worked in the administrative office, I could probably sweet talk him into getting me out of it. Well, it was worth a shot. Jumping up to my feet, I snatched the schedule back from Trina and started for the door.

"Where are you going?" Trina called after me.

I waved the paper in the air. "What do you think?"

I heard Trina's laughter all the way down the hallway. However, the good mood I was in slowly seeped out of me as the eyes trailed after me. Now, these weren't the usual stares I'd gotten when I first came. You know, the curious ones every new kid got. They weren't even the ones of fearful worship from after I beat down Sabrina. No, these stares said they had dirt, dirt on me.

As soon as I hit the quad, it didn't take me long to find someone to tell me what was going on. "Hey, Steph!"

I came up beside a freckle-faced ginger which I had Potions with last semester. She had her phone out holding it up for another girl I didn't know to see. When I called her name, however, she quickly put her phone down, and a guilty look crossed her face.

“Hey, Max.” She shifted in place, fidgeting with the bangs of her pixie cut hair. “This is Victoria.” Stephanie pointed a thumb at the girl beside her.

I gave her a polite nod but stayed focused on Stephanie. Crossing my arms over my chest, I inclined my head to her phone. “Want to tell me what everyone is so ‘The Hills Have Eyes’ about today?”

“Nothing.” Stephanie quickly shook her head. “It’s nothing really.”

Sighing at her reluctance, I fingered the necklace around my neck. Why wouldn’t she just tell me? My day had already started out crappy with the whole P.E. thing hanging in the balance, I didn’t need more crap on my plate right now.

Before I realized the words coming out of my mouth, I said, “I wish you would just tell me.” The necklace around my neck warmed, and I immediately knew what I had done. The one day I decided to wear my dad’s present, and I already use a wish. In all hindsight, I probably should have just used it to get out of P.E., not to get to the bottom of some rumor.

It didn’t take very long for Steph to start talking after I made my wish. “It’s been circulating all morning, not just through text but on social media too. People are hashtagging it all over.”

She shoved her phone at me, showing me an image of Ian and me kissing, the one I knew Sabrina had taken. However, it wasn't the image that made my blood boil but the caption with it.

#MancasterPrincess or #MancasterWhore? Looks like our resident queen has added another willing victim to her collection.

Wonderful. I was in the middle of a freaking Teen Drama centered around me and my love life. Did people not have lives?

"I'm really sorry." Steph stared at me with sympathy or pity. Either way, I didn't like it.

"Don't worry about it." I gritted my teeth and gave her the phone back. Suddenly, all the eyes on me made sense. I had a feeling they were only second away from making buttons and t-shirts spouting what side they were on.

Stalking away from Steph, I headed toward the administration office. My mood only got worse with each step I took and the more whispers and stares I got. By the time I entered the glass doors and weaved around the long line, I was burning mad.

"Dale!" I shouted, strutting into the administrator's office like I owned the place. My eyes immediately found the reddish mop of hair as it jerked up from the student he was assisting.

A curious expression crossed his face, much like those who were watching me make a scene before he pushed his black-rimmed glasses up his nose and received me with a bland tone. "If you would like my assistance, I would be happy to help you ..." I opened my mouth to snap that he better hope to hell he would when he gestured to the line. "... when it's your turn."

I glanced at the line and then back at him, at the line again, then him before letting out a growl. "Are you serious?"

Dale tapped a pen on the top of his desk and nodded curtly.

Seeing I wasn't going to get anywhere coming in here like a child throwing a temper tantrum, which I had been, I crossed my arms over my chest and stepped to the back of the line. If a pin dropped, it could be heard in the deafening silence that followed my and Dale's interaction. That was until Dale began to speak to the student in front of him again. Then the cell phones came out, and there were hushed murmurs and not so discreet looks in my direction.

Great. I wanted less attention on myself, and here I was, adding fuel to the fire. Sabrina would be rolling in glee at the avalanche of rumors she had begun.

I stood in line, tapping my finger against my arm as it moved at snail pace. It was like people didn't want to leave because they wanted to see the explosion that would bound to happen once I hit the front of the line. They weren't wrong, the irritation in me that had more to do with the rumors being spread than the actual reason I was there only grew as the time ticked by.

Ten minutes. I stood in line for ten minutes before I finally arrived before Dale and had my day in court, so to speak.

"What's this bullshit?" I slapped the copy of my schedule on the counter in front of me before he had a second to get a word in edgewise.

"Language," Dale calmly stated before taking the paper from me and adding so low that those behind us strained to hear, "before I find another use for that dirty mouth of yours."

My shoulders hunched up to my ears and my face flamed. "Not now, fox boy."

Dale's ears peeked, and he glanced up at me with an amused quirk of his lips. "Fox-boy?"

I scowled, gesturing at his face. "You know, fox boy. Red hair, angular face, a sneaky brown-noser." I sniffed, sticking my nose in the air.

Clearing his throat, Dale fingered my class schedule without meeting my gaze. "I'm not sure if I should be offended or flattered."

"Sounds like an insult to me." The guy behind me in line decided to put his two cents in.

I shot a glare back at him which didn't do much of anything. Note to self, work on death glare.

"In any case," Dale interrupted my attempt to kill the guy with my eyes, drawing my attention back to him. "I fail to see what the problem is?"

"My schedule." I tapped the paper until my finger hurt.

"Yes," Dale drew out, innocent as could be. "What about it?"

Getting tired of his coyness, I picked it up and shoved it at his face. "Read it."

Taking the paper from my hands and lowering it, he sighed. "I did. Since I was the one who typed it up. Hence the reason I do not see an issue. These are all required courses for you to progress to your next year."

Frustrated that he still wasn't getting it, I spelled it out for him. "P.E., Dale? Really? I thought I was done with that crap when I graduated high school." A few sniggers from the line behind me made me twist around and glower. This time they quieted promptly, though it didn't stop them from snapping pictures and texting. Really, didn't they have anything better to do?

Dale rubbed his temple and leaned an elbow on the top of the counter. "Physical Education is just as important for your magical education as it is for your body. We here are Winchester

Academy believe that with a sound mind and a sound body ..."

I jumped slightly and twisted around as the rest of the line behind me joined in his words like some creepy cult. "... makes for sound magic."

Staring at the people like they had all drunk the purple Kool-Aid, something no one in their right mind would do, seriously. Grapes were only good for eating whole and wine, never a food flavoring. Scowling, I eased back around to Dale.

"That's all great and stuff, but I'm not a runner. Or a worker-outer. I'm a downward dog kind of girl." The guy next to me made a sound that earned him a death glare from Dale this time. At least, I knew the guy had my back on one level. "If I wanted to torture myself, I'd join a gym."

"I understand your hesitancy," Dale started and turned slightly to the next guy in line as if already dismissing me, but I wasn't going to have it.

"No, you don't." I slapped my hand on the counter, bringing his attention back to me. "I signed up to come to this place to learn how to keep myself from killing myself or those around me, not to get in shape, which I might add I haven't had any complaints from you so far." I shoved a finger at his chest with a growl. "The only reason I will ever run is because zombies have, as they inevitably will, broken out and are chasing my fine ass," I smacked my backside for good measure, so they were aware of how unworried I was about getting fat, then added as an afterthought, "or there's a two for one sale on shoes. So, thank you but no."

Dale stared at me for a moment and then took his glasses off. He pulled a piece of cloth from his pocket and began to rub it across his lenses. "Are you quite finished?"

Having lost most of my steam, I nodded. "Yeah. I'm done."

"Very well." Dale lifted his glasses to the light as he looked through them and then placed them back on his face. "The class is mandatory. I can't do anything about it. If you have that much of an aversion, you can bring it up with the headmaster."

My eyes darted to the headmaster's door and pouted. "Really?"

Dale quirked a brow.

"Fine." Sighing dejectedly, I grabbed my schedule and slogged away from the counter.

"That's it?" The guy next in line cried out. "After all that, and you aren't even going to wail on him or show any of your powers?"

Before I could answer him, Dale came around the desk and took my arm, pulling me flush against him. I could feel more than hear the phones coming out as they seemed obsessed with doing lately as Dale cupped my face with one hand. That was all the warning I had before his mouth crashed onto mine and the murmurs and click of cameras all fell away.

My hand clutched Dale's arm the muscle beneath the shirt flex under my touch. His tongue buried in between my lips wrapping it around mine. I angled my head to the side, opening up for him, but as abruptly as the kiss started, it ended, leaving me breathless and light headed.

"What was that for?" I breathed, wiping the edges of my mouth and promptly ignoring the crowd of students staring at us.

"Proving a point." Dale traced his thumb along the edge of my lip before pressing it to his mouth, tasting me. It was the hottest thing I had ever seen in my life, and if my knees had not already been rubbery, they sure were now.

I blinked up at his answer and then it clicked. The picture. Sabrina. Of course, he had seen it. It answered why he had been so curt with me in the first place, but not why he had kissed me in front of everyone. I'd think he'd want to be as far away from me as possible not add to the #*MancasterWhore* bit.

"But I ..."

"Well, talk about it later." Dale dipped his head and headed back to his table, calling for the next person in line, leaving me dumbfounded in the middle of the office area.

After a moment, I shook my head and headed for the door. I caught sight of a few people's screens as I went past. I should have been angry that they had taken such a private thing of me and were sharing it around, but the image of Dale with his arms around me did funny things to my insides, and not one of them was bad.

Chapter 7

TRINA HADN'T BEEN LYING about Etiquette of Magic being a snooze-fest. I had a hard time keeping my eyes open regardless of the fact that the instructor was a Clark Kent type and less than thirty, two things that none of my previous professors had been. However, as pretty as his face and ass were to look at, his voice made a robot sound interesting.

Even Callie would have had a tough time staying awake.

"If you take anything away from this class," Professor Morison droned on, his voice as energized as a cup of Sleepy Time Tea, "it is that the magical community comes from a long line of traditions. Those traditions must be upheld. No matter how asinine you may find them in this modern age." Morison smiled, a little quirk of the lips that had most of the females sighing dreamily.

All except me.

I was too busy wiping the drool off my chin and hoping no one snapped a picture. If I didn't see another image of me on social media, it would be too soon.

As Morison dismissed class, my phone buzzed. I gathered my bag and glanced down at my phone, only to groan.

Callie: Want to tell me why exactly you're trending?

"Fuck!" I slammed my hand down on the table startling the remaining students. I waved them off and glared down at my phone as I tried to figure out how my bestie could have possibly found out about my new infamy.

Me: I'll tell you about it later.

"Something upsetting you, Ms. Norman?" Morison tapped his fingers on the tabletop in front of me.

For having a monotone, sleep-inducing voice, he did gain points for calling me by my requested last name and not just assuming I wanted to go by Mancaster. My eyes narrowed at the lingering students who immediately headed for the door the moment I looked their way.

When we were alone, Morison moved to the door and closed it, giving us privacy. "You have become something of a celebrity, it seems, in your brief time here, Ms. Norman."

I gaped at Morison as he scratched the side of his face and walked toward me. Gone was the monotone voice and in its place was a melt-your-panties English accent that would have had me drooling earlier for a completely different reason.

"Why, uh, how...?" I gaped at him, trying to figure out what the heck just happened.

Morison leaned his elbows on the tall laboratory table in front of us, a sneaky grin on his luscious lips. "I can understand the confusion you must be feeling right now. To clear things up, yes, I always sound like this. The other voice is a ploy to make my students pay attention to my class and not what I look like naked."

I nodded dumbly. "Completely, understandable."

"I trust you can keep this secret between the two of us?" He gestured a finger between us with a raised brow.

"Yeah, I mean, yes. Of course. My lips are sealed." I mimed doing just that, going so far as to lock them and throw away the key.

"Good." Morison tapped the table with a renewed energy. "So, now that you know my secret, how about you let me in on what is troubling you?"

I sagged in my chair, collapsing my head onto my folded arms, and groaned. "I'm a freaking hashtag."

"Excuse me?"

I lifted my head when I realized my words had been muffled by the table. "I'm a hashtag. As in people on social media are talking about me and my choice of boyfriends, and I do mean that plurally." I lowered my lids until they were slits as I dared him to question my morals or call me a slut for my choices.

"Is that all?" Morison smirked, leaning his face on his hand, looking way more interested than he should about a student's social life. "Well, your life hasn't been lived if you aren't the center of some kind of melodrama."

"But I don't want to be famous for anything. I just want to do my class work, keep my magic from blowing someone up, and not get bullied for not being a dick." I made a face and shot daggers as my phone buzzed once more. This time the screen lit up with my grandmother's number and not the good one.

"Do you need to get that?"

"No." I sagged in my seat. I knew exactly why she would be calling me. Nothing traveled faster than bad news. The fact that my own mother hadn't seen it yet surprised me, though she might have and just laughed it off. "I do need to get to my next class though." I stood from my seat and shoved my phone in my back pocket. "Thanks for listening."

Morison straightened and followed me to the door. "It was my pleasure. And Max?" My eyes trailed down to the hand on my shoulder and then back up to Morison's slate-grey eyes. "You'll keep my secret?"

"Of course." I nodded, expecting that to be the end of it.

"Good. I also expect next time that you will stay awake at least for half of my class?" He arched a brow, and I flushed with embarrassment. "You even have permission to stare at my ass if you like. I've been told it is quite drool-worthy."

My mouth gaped open as Morison opened the door and ushered me outside. I was still partially in a daze when a hand clamped down on my arm making me jump in place.

"Jumpy?"

My head swiveled so fast, I feared it might fall off. It might have been better if it had since today was just full of fun surprises. The large broad shoulders of the man beside me actually happened to be in the pleasant variety. At least, I knew he wouldn't talk my ear off about the rumors.

I hoped.

"Aidan. How are you?" My eyes crinkled as I angled my head back to look up at the mountain of a man. His hands, which were as big as my face, were tucked into the pockets of his jeans, his emerald green t-shirt strained against the massive muscles beneath causing the video game character on the front to distort its shape. Azure eyes gleamed at me with curiosity, and a hint of amusement tinged his lips.

"Good. You?"

Those two words alone caused a shiver down my spine, the kind that settled low in between my thighs and made me clear my throat. "I'm okay, all things considered."

Not waiting for him to figure out what I was talking about, I started toward the library. I'd told Morison I had class, but I wasn't sure I could handle listening to people whispering about me when they thought the professor wasn't looking, no matter how interesting Alchemy Through the Ages sounded.

"Do you have class now?"

"No."

Aidan continued to walk along beside me as if he had nowhere else to be but near me. It was sweet but also kind of creepy especially since he didn't talk much. Maybe he was shy?

I chewed on my upper lip as I thought of what to say. He liked video games, I could start with that. Except I couldn't even figure out *Tetris*, let alone whatever hardcore gaming he was in. I was lucky to recognize the character on his shirt had to do with games.

"Library."

"Huh?" My eyes shot up from where I had been staring at the ground as we walked. The tile really wasn't that interesting, but it was better than counting all the eyes staring at me.

“I’m heading to the library.”

“Oh.” Slightly surprised by the number of words he had actually said to me, it took me a moment to find a comprehensible response. “I’m heading there too.”

“I know.”

I stopped and put my hand out, forcing Aidan to stop or run into my arm. “What do you mean, you know? I didn’t tell anyone where I was going.” Suddenly, his showing up and following me made him seem less ‘cute shy guy’ and more ‘stalker about to get hit in the nuts.’

I glared up at him waiting for him to explain himself. Aidan didn’t seem at all bothered. He actually went so far as to raise his brow at me and then took my hand still pressed against his chest into his grasp.

Turning my hand over, his thumb brushed along the lines of my hand causing a tremble to rush through me. I jerked my hand away from him and rubbed it on my pants, trying to force the tingles away.

“I don’t intend to harm you, Max,” Aidan’s voice boomed through the hallway and those lingering stopped in their tracks to watch us.

“Then what do you want?”

“To be by your side.” Aidan peered down at me, the intensity of his gaze making me squirm.

Crossing my arms over my chest, I tapped my foot. “While I am appreciative of your help at the Halloween Mixer, I don’t have any room in my life for a stalker. So, if you don’t mind, go find someone else to blink those pretty blue eyes at.”

Aidan’s lips twitched. “I’m psychic, not a stalker.”

“Psychic?” My eyes widened, and then I leaned toward him and whispered, “Can you read my thoughts?”

The deep chuckle that rumbled through Aidan made my thighs press together tightly. “That would be a telepath. I have precognitive abilities.”

“So, you can see the future?” I squinted at him, my brow scrunching so hard together that it was pinching my skin.

“Small amounts.” Aidan nodded.

“Like where I’m going to be.” I narrowed my eyes at him, not completely reassured that he wasn’t stalking me.

Aidan ducked his head slightly, his cheeks coloring a faint pink. It was strange and yet adorable to see on such a beefy man. “It does have its perks.”

“Like knowing where I’m at all the time?” I twisted on my heel and started toward the library once more. “I’m not sure I like you knowing where I’m at. How do I know you don't see other things? Like when I'm in the shower or changing?"

"I would never." Aidan caught up with me without much effort. Must be nice to have such long legs. "I wished to see you, but I am not without honor."

"Honor, huh?" I leaned my head toward him, my eyes rolling up to meet his. "That's pretty fourteenth century of you, don't you think?"

Aidan simply smiled, a small quirk of the lips that started those tingles again. To distract myself, I turned and dug into my bag. I spent more time than I needed finding the book I wanted while I hoped Aidan would stop staring at me like he wanted to take me home to his mother.

"Well," I cleared my throat and pointed a book toward the library doors. "I'm going to head on in, you can join me... you know, if you want to."

I didn't wait to see if he would follow. I pushed through the library doors and headed toward the table in the back that I had claimed as my own. Unfortunately, I wasn't safe from the stares and whispers here either. However, the large shadow casting over me had the majority of them shutting up on the spot.

Sliding into a chair, I flipped open my book. Aidan took the seat across from me, no book or anything else to occupy him. He laced his hands on the table and watched... me.

Shifting in my seat, I tried to ignore him. Since I was missing the Alchemy class, I figured I'd better get the reading in. However, with the exception of some guy named Roger Bacon, a horribly tragic name for an alchemist, I couldn't make myself focus on the words in front of me.

My head jerked up from my book. I slapped my hands on the table and scowled. "Are you just going to sit there and stare at me? Don't you have better things to do? Like, look ahead at where I'll be tomorrow?"

Aidan's eyes narrowed, but I wasn't going to be intimidated. I locked eyes with him and did a silent cheer when he looked away first.

"My abilities do not work that way."

"Well, then please enlighten me." I waved a hand in his direction, leaning back and crossing one leg over the other.

Instead of explaining his superhero powers that frankly I was finding ridiculous, he simply stared off to the right of my head. What the hell was up with this crap? There were witches and wizards. Potions and spells. This wasn't some storybook, there had to be a line somewhere, right?

I let out a long audible sigh, dropping my arms to fall beside me as I angled my head back to silently curse at the ceiling. Just as I was about to get back to finding out what kind of sick parent would name their kid Roger Bacon, Aidan spoke.

"Paul Broomstein will be joining us."

"Huh?" I straightened in my seat and twisted around looking for the younger of the two Broomsteins. While Ian had made sure I remembered him seconds after I arrived on campus, I hadn't seen or heard from Paul. Not that I was anxiously waiting for his arrival or anything. I'm not that kind of girl. Really, I'm not.

"I think your crystal ball is broken." I gave Aidan a pointed look, collapsing back in my seat.

Aidan's face said he was not amused by my snark. Too bad for him. I was hilarious, and there was more where that came from.

"Max." The sound of Paul's voice and I was up on my feet. Down, girl. Sit down. Someone smelled of desperation.

I stretched my arms over my head and yawned, turning slightly until I saw Paul. "Paul. Hi. I didn't see you there."

Aidan snorted, and I shot him a warning look before taking my seat once more. "Still doesn't prove anything."

"What?" Paul asked, sitting next to me at the table.

I shook my head, my eyes lingering on Aidan before I turned to Paul. "Nothing. So, fancy seeing you here."

"Yeah." Paul ran a hand through his mahogany hair. Just a touch shade lighter than his brothers, his eyes staring down at the table. "I'm sorry I haven't been in touch. I had a—"

"Teacher's assistant thing." I nodded at him. "Yeah, Ian told me you didn't come home for the holiday." I tried to keep the disappointment out of my voice, but I didn't succeed.

"Right, well, I wasn't avoiding him or anything. Just I had already signed up for the extra credit before the whole..." He rolled his hand in the air in front of him as he searched for his words.

"I got it." Clucking my tongue, I glanced over at Aidan who watched with increasing amusement before bumping my foot against Paul's. "Hey, I'm famous now, you know? And not just for kicking Sabrina's ass last semester."

Paul grinned and withdrew his phone from his back pocket. Flipping through the screen, he didn't show me the picture that I thought he would of Ian and me, but the one of Dale and me in the office. This time the caption this time read, *#MancasterWhore strikes again.*

I grimaced. "Well, no one can ever say I'm not photogenic."

"You guys make a cute couple." Paul inclined his head and put his phone on the table. "Ian too."

I reached out a hand and touched Paul's arm. "I'm not sure what you heard, but I'm not just cycling through guys. I genuinely like you and them." Aidan made a growling kind of sound, and I shot my gaze his way. "Sometimes you, but the point is that I'm not what they are making me out to be."

Paul placed his hand on top of mine and gave it a squeeze. "I know. Don't you think I'd know Sabrina's work anywhere? She's lashing out for you taking her power, and this is the only way she knows how to fight. Dirty."

I let out a cross between a laugh and a choking cough. "Yeah, well, she doesn't know who she's dealing with. I'm not going to be beaten by some high school teen drama crap. We're grown adults and can do what we want."

"Exactly." Paul grinned, his hand coming out to pinch my chin between his forefinger and thumb. I let him lead me toward him until our lips pressed against one another. This time I wasn't kissing him, because he was sad and I wanted him to feel better. This time, I was kissing him because I damn well wanted to, everyone else be damned.

"Trouble is coming." Aidan's warning was a fraction of a second too late before the Wicked Witch of Winchester Academy herself came thundering into the library.

Chapter 8

AIDAN STOOD FROM HIS seat and maneuvered around the table to lean on the corner beside. His move suggested he thought to protect me in some way from Sabrina. However nice the sentiment, I hardly thought he could do much to save me. I did that pretty well on my own.

Paul tried to shift closer to me as well, but hurricane Sabrina launched herself between us. She hopped up on the table, forcing us to shift back or get kicked in the face by her three-inch heels. One long tanned leg crossed over the other, her skirt barely covering her backside. How she moved around without flashing anyone must have been some kind of magic, the kind I'd never have.

"I missed you this Christmas," Sabrina cooed, reaching out a hand to brush Paul's hair behind his ear. He jerked away at the touch, making her pout. "The holiday wasn't the same without you this year. Daddy asked about you, you know."

Shifting uncomfortably, Paul flicked his eyes my direction before answering her. "I was busy."

Instead of causing Sabrina to throw a fit, she actually smiled. This one promised she had a secret and she wasn't even a bit sorry to spill it. "I heard about your little assignment over the break, seems your brother had no problem swooping in while you were away." She sighed dramatically, giving me a sly glance. "Just like Ian to take what he wants when no one is looking."

I bristled and started toward her, but Aidan's hand clamped down on my shoulder. Shooting him a glare, I jerked my attention back to Sabrina, but Paul had already jumped in for me.

"You don't know what you are talking about. I suggest you leave well enough alone and mind your own business." Paul's voice was firm and held no room for argument, not that it stopped Sabrina.

Throwing her head back so that her long blond hair cascaded over her shoulders – did she practice this crap in the mirror or what? – she met our questioning looks with a vicious grin. "Did you really think I would let some bottom feeder like her make a fool of you and me?" She bumped Paul's knee with the heel of her shoe. “You deserve so much better than her, someone who will give you their full attention. Not someone who will open her cauldron to just anyone who waves their wand in her direction.”

I rolled my eyes at her analogy and was about to counter her childish quips, but Aidan beat me to it.

“We do not use wands.”

Pressing my lips together tightly, I fought against the need to laugh, but the confused expression on Sabrina’s face just did me in. Curling over in my seat as I laughed, I rubbed the back of my hand over my watering eyes. Paul’s lips curled up at the edges as if he wanted to laugh as well but knew better than me to indulge. I, however, did not give a rat’s ass.

“Is he retarded or what?” Sabrina pointed a finger at Aidan, and my laughter died.

Growling, I pushed against Aidan’s hand and stood. I had no doubt he had let me stand up, or I’d be back in that seat so fast, I’d have wood burn on my ass. Placing one hand on the table, I leaned toward Sabrina so that our eyes met. “Don’t ever speak to him again.”

Sabrina’s eyes narrowed, and she smirked. “Or what? You’ll use your puny little powers on me again?” She glanced away from me for a moment, and the curve of her lips widened. “Please do. I’d love nothing more than proof that you do not belong at this school or in our world."

My head pivoted away from her and toward where she stared. The library's occupants had stopped their studying and had full on started to observe us. Once more the phones were out and no doubt recording our whole little scene. Snarling in frustration, I whipped my face back to hers.

"You think you can beat me?" I cocked my head to the side. "With petty rumors and traps? I mean, I already bested you with magic, something I only learned eight months ago. I guess it shows how desperate you are."

Instead of fury filling her eyes like I had hoped, Sabrina simply grinned. She hopped off the table, forcing me to move back and then proceeded to wrap herself around Paul. "I don't need magic to get rid of you, you're doing a fantastic job yourself. And Paul here," a manicured hand patted his chest, and her lip poked out, her lashes batting at him, "is just a victim of your siren call. It's only a matter of time before they recognize you for the harpy that you are and when that happens, I'll be here." She pressed her lips to his cheek, leaving an imprint of pink lipstick there.

A part of me wondered why Paul hadn't shoved her out of his lap. Why did he let her paw at him in front of all those people? Did what she said ring true for him? Was I really leading them all to their doom? But one glance down at his hands and I had my answer.

His hands curled around the chair's handles, turning his knuckles white. With any luck, he was two seconds away from upending her onto the floor in front of all those cameras pointing our way. Give her a taste of her own medicine.

Unfortunately, my hopes never came to fruition. Sabrina stood to her feet, giving Paul one last sultry look before she stalked away.

I gaped after her. She was just going to sashay over her, threaten me, insult me, maul my guy, and then walk away? I don't think so.

Without saying anything, I stalked after her. My legs did double time catching up, and I half expected my unrequested bodyguard would stop me. The thought of Aidan coming between us spurred my feet forward until I could stretch my hand out and grasp Sabrina's arm, pulling her to a stop.

"What the hell?" Sabrina screeched loud enough that if the students in the library weren't already zeroed in on us, they would be now. "Let me go, you freak."

I tightened my grip until she winced, but unlike her, I kept my voice low. "No, you listen to me. I might have embarrassed you in front of everyone, I admit that, but you started this. I just wanted to be a normal girl. I never asked for a magical education, but I wouldn't give it up for anything in the world now."

Sabrina sniffed indignantly. "Of course not, why would anyone want to be normal?"

My nails pinched into her skin, hinting that she should shut up now. "However, if you ever, and I mean ever, try to touch Paul or any of my guys again and I will make you wish you had never met me." I brought our faces so close that bystanders probably thought we were flirting. "Are we clear?"

Frowning so hard that lines formed around her mouth, Sabrina bit out, "Fine. Now get your grubby paws off me."

Not quite believing her but satisfied I got my point across, I released her. I didn't get more than a few steps away before she opened her big mouth again.

"He was mine first, you know. He will be mine again."

Fingering the necklace around my neck, I sighed, and my head drooped. Why couldn't she leave well enough alone? Turning back around, I shook my head slowly. "You can't take a hint, can you? Paul doesn't want you. You messed up. Own up to it and move on."

"I can't." She crossed her arms over her chest and lifted her chin defiantly.

Backing away from her but not turning my back, I said, "I wish you'd just find someone else to hit on. Maybe it'll help you get over him because this...” I gestured up and down her form. “... isn’t helping.”

The necklace warmed beneath my fingers, and Sabrina straightened like an arrow. Almost zombie-like, her eyes wide and her face slack, she spun on her heels and went up to the closest person, which happened to be a gawking brunette girl, and promptly punched her in the face.

The whole room erupted in chaos over the action. The girl’s nose spurt blood everywhere, causing her friends to rush to her side. They shoved Sabrina back who had a look of confusion on her face before she realized what she had done. Then those blazing blue eyes of her zeroed in on me.

Not waiting for the other shoe to drop, I hurried back to my bag. Shoving everything into it, I ignored the questioning looks from Aidan and Paul, more so from Aidan than Paul. That big lug head had more going on in his noggin than he led on.

“Where are you going?” Paul stood and followed after me. I dashed around the crowd in the middle of the library and zipped around stacks of books. One glance back told me only Paul had followed. I didn’t have to wonder why Aidan hadn’t. If he had precognitive abilities like he claimed, he’d find me before long.

“To lunch. I’m hungry.” My stomach rumbled as if to collaborate my story. I pushed through the library doors with Paul still hot on my heels. A hand slid into mine and pulled me toward the direction of the cafeteria.

"Good." Paul grinned. "I'm buying."

Chapter 9

PAUL BYPASSED THE CAFETERIA and led me out through the back of the campus toward a small gated entrance I'd never used before.

"Where are we going?" I shot a curious look at the single guard at this entrance who only gave Paul and me a nod before letting us through. Paul held onto my elbow as he brought me over to a black Jeep Patriot. He opened the door for me, giving me a hand in before rounding the vehicle.

Paul started the car and fiddled with the radio before settling on a popular rock station. He pulled out of the driveway before turning, angling his chin toward me. "What do you feel like?"

My brows scrunched down, and I frowned hard. "I don't know. Freaked out and a bit confused."

Paul chuckled, the sound making my insides curl deliciously, as he glanced away from the road to me. “I mean, food. What do you want to eat?”

“Oh.” I sank down into the chair and stared out the window. “I don’t know. Anything is fine. I’m not really hungry.”

“Well, I am, and using magic like that?” Paul whistled and laughed once more. “That kind of power can work up an appetite.”

I ignored Paul’s little dig and clutched my necklace closer to me. The first two wishes I had made, I had blown off as coincidence.

I wanted someone to kiss me at midnight. Callie called Dale. Easy, right? That’s what I had thought.

Then there was the whole thing with Steph. I’d like to think it was my charm and wit that had her giving me her phone when I asked. However, wishing she’d just tell me pretty much killed that idea.

Now in the library, I couldn’t even pretend I had caused Sabrina to have a change of heart. Maybe my words had gotten to her? I made her have some kind of mental break, and she lashed out at the first person she saw. However, that look of surprise that showed up on her face said that was no truer than anything else I’d thought up.

I didn’t know why I didn’t believe the amulet would actually work. My parents wouldn’t give me something that wasn’t real. I shouldn’t have played with it like it was some toy. It was magical. Magic had consequences. Except it was the student in the library with a bloody nose that ended up having to pay for my carelessness.

"So, are you going to tell me? Or is it some big secret?"

Paul's voice jolted me out of my thoughts, and I shifted in my seat. I dragged a hand through my hair and leaned against the door. "It's not a secret, I guess. And it wasn't me. Well," I fiddled with the amulet and glanced over at Paul, "maybe a little bit."

"That's new."

The moment his eyes landed on the necklace, I dropped it. "It doesn't matter."

"Come on. You've got me interested now." His lips quirked up on the corners. "Gift from Callie? A boyfriend?" Paul's voice held a hard edge to it.

I smirked. Jealous much?

"More like my parents." I shoved my bag under the seat as we parked in the parking lot of one of the many sub shops near the school. The scent of freshly baked bread filled my senses the moment I opened the car door. My stomach rumbled. Guess I was a bit hungry.

"That's nice of them." Paul met me at the front of the car and took my hand, leading me toward the shop. His hand was warm and slightly damp in mine but still made something in me squeal with glee. Paul was not so subtle, telling people I was his. Kind of like how Dale had but with less tongue.

We stopped at the back of the line, waiting to put our order in. Paul released my hand so that he could lean against the railing, his arms crossed over his chest. "Do your parents give you a lot of presents like that?"

I shook my head. "No, this is the first magical gift they've given me. Of course, it was the first holiday we've celebrated since I found out I'm a witch."

We shifted further in the line. Paul tucked his hands in his pockets and ducked his head. "Our parents don't really do the whole holiday thing, not since we were kids. Even then, our nannies were the ones who woke us up for presents they'd picked out for us and wrapped for our parents." The sadness in his eyes made me want to wrap my arms around him and hold him tight.

"It's a wishing amulet." I spat out for no reason other than he was sad and I wanted to change the subject. Paul's eyes shot to me as well as the teenager behind the sub counter. I fingered the amulet and leaned in closer to him. "My parents got it for me in Cairo."

Paul raised a brow but didn't comment. He told the teenager what he wanted and then glanced over at me. I mumbled my order, and we shifted further up the line. He grabbed my hand once more bringing me close to his side.

A weird feeling overcame me, kind of like when you're in a plane and your ears needed to pop. It made all the noise in the shop faded into the background.

"So, a wishing amulet." Paul turned to me with a smile. "Like one of those you have ten wishes kind of wishing amulets?"

"Yeah," I said slowly, cocking my head to the side as I realized no one was paying any mind to the fact that Paul was talking nonsense. "What did you just do?"

"Privacy spell." Paul brought our hands up in front of us as he turned to face me. "Have you been making a lot of wishes this month?"

I shook my head. "No, not really. I mean, not on purpose."

"How many are we talking about then?"

My shoulders reached my ears as I stared at the ground. "Three."

"And one of those was for Sabrina to punch someone?" The way Paul's mouth curled up at the thought of Sabrina hitting that girl made my heart beat faster. What was it about these guys that had my hormones going haywire?

"No," I scowled. "I didn't wish for Sabrina to hit someone. That was just a side effect of my telling her to stop hitting on you." My cheeks burned with embarrassment.

"Really now?" The male satisfaction that was on his face made me want to hit him at the same time as I wanted to lay one on him.

Before I could decide which one I was going to do, my phone went off.

I glanced down at my phone and saw Dale's name flash over the screen. "Uh, hold that thought." I held a finger up as I pressed the answer button. "Hello?"

"Hey, where are you?" Dale's voice had a sense of urgency to it.

"I'm having lunch with Paul." Paul shot me a grin and wink just as the person behind the counter called our number.

"Well, you better cut it short. The headmaster wants to see you. Now." There wasn't any jealousy or irritation in his voice, like Dale wasn't happy I was out with Paul. It was more like worry, worry for me.

I swallowed thickly and nodded. When I remembered he couldn't see me, I said into the phone, "Okay, yeah. I'll be there in a few." Dale started to hang up, but I stopped him. "Hey, Dale. Is it bad?"

The frustrated rush of air that came out was not encouraging. "I'm not sure. You should just get here. Soon."

He hung up before I could ask anything else. I frowned at the phone as Paul came up to me with our food in his hands. "Better get that for the road, my quick getaway was not so discreet as I hoped."

Paul sighed and turned back to the counter. He got a bag for our food, and we headed back to the car. The ride back to the school was tense. What did the headmaster want? Had Sabrina tattled on me? Or was it something else?

"I'm sure everything will be fine," Paul reassured me with a squeeze of my hand. I gave him a weak smile before he hopped out of his side of the car and came around to help me out. He led me back through the special entrance I could only assume was for teachers and faculty, teacher's assistant apparently counted for something more than extra work, and then through the quad.

I should have been used to the feel of eyes on my back by now, but it was just as bad as this morning. Whether they were staring and whispering because of what happened in the library or because of my new infamy on social media, I didn't know or care. They didn't have a say in my continuing attendance at the school.

Paul came with me as I walked into the administrator's office. Thankfully, for once, there was no line at Dale's counter, but a few people were sitting in some chairs off to the side. Dale approached me the moment I came through the door. His eyes darted to Paul, and the guys exchanged a look of male understanding before he drew me toward him.

"What exactly happened in the library?" Dale's hushed tone made me know that I had not gotten away scott free.

My eyes moved to the people sitting in the waiting area and then back to Dale. Lifting a shoulder, I shook my head slightly. "Nothing really, just Sabrina's usual 'I'm the queen of the campus so I can do whatever I want' bullshit."

"So, you didn't cast a spell on her to make her punch the headmaster's niece?"

I winced. The headmaster's niece? Fuck me. As much as I hated to kill the hopefulness in his voice, I couldn't beat around the bush with this. "I didn't put a spell on her."

Dale's shoulders sagged.

"But I did wish she'd hit on someone else."

A curse escaped Dale's lips just as the door to the headmaster's office opened. Sabrina came striding out with a cat that ate the canary grin on her lips. She took one look at me, and my guys and an evil glint was added to that grin.

"Well, well, look who it is. The Mancaster Whore and her lap dogs." She shoved her way between us until she could brush her hands against Paul's chest in passing. "You let me know when you're tired of playing second fiddle to, well ..." she giggled, her eyes going to Dale. "Everyone."

I glared daggers into her back, praying that she would trip over her own feet. However, the gods were not listening to me today. I had a feeling they hadn't been listening to me for a while now, or I wouldn't be in this mess.

Before I could comment on Sabrina's nasty comments, the headmaster's voice came over the intercom at Dale's desk. "Send Miss Norman in, please."

Dale touched my shoulder, his lips pressed thinly into a line. Paul held onto my hand, bringing it up to his lips. His mouth brushed against the top of it. In normal circumstances, I'd have been hot and bothered by the action. Right now, though, I was more worried about saving my own ass than getting some.

I nodded at the two of them and let out a hard breath. It was now or never.

Headmaster Swordson sat behind his desk, a somber expression on his aged face. He seemed to have aged quite a bit since I had last sat in here, talking to him about what last name I wanted to go by. The grey in his hair was a duller shade and the lines on his face had deepened considerably. I hoped the stress he was enduring was not from me and something else entirely. I clung to the fact that he still called me by Norman rather than my grandparents' last name. I thought it told me he still respected me and if that were the case, then I couldn't be in that much trouble.

“Please have a seat.” Headmaster Swordson glanced up from his desk to gesture weakly toward the chair in front of him.

I did as he asked, my heart beating rapidly in my chest. I waited for the headmaster to start in on me. Accusing me of whatever Sabrina said I did, which by Dale’s words, I’d put a spell on her. However, the headmaster didn’t look like he wanted to be here any more than me, and when he didn’t say anything for several moments but stared at a picture frame on his desk, I cleared my throat.

“Headmaster?”

His eyes darted up to me, and he looked at me like he had forgotten I was there. “Miss Norman. The semester has barely started, and already you are the talk of the school.”

“About that,” I scooched forward in my seat, determined to get my side out before he could slam down the punishment. “I didn’t do—”

The headmaster put his hand up, cutting me off. “I’m not interested in knowing the details. Miss Craftsman already painted me a very ugly picture. One that I’m sure has a different hue coming from you.”

I gaped at him.

He smiled slightly, a bare twitch of the lips. “I didn’t get the position as headmaster by not being good at maneuvering the politics and the students with those politically inclined parents.” Meaning Sabrina and the rest of the privileged crew, which would also include me had I cared about my grandparents' crap.

"So, if you don't care what's going on then why am I here?" My leg bounced as I started to get nervous for a whole different reason.

"I asked you here because I have found myself in the position of mediator. One that I do not mind being in but would like to remind you that your family matters should stay that way. In the family." Before I could respond the door behind me opened, and Dale ushered in my grandparents.

The apologetic look on Dale's face told me he didn't know anything about it. I begged him with my eyes to get me out of this, but unfortunately, my grandmother not so subtle shoved him out of the room, clear disapproval in her frown.

My grandfather thankfully didn't seem as peeved as she was, and boy, was my grandmother pissed. If I thought she had a rod up her ass before, nothing compared to the tightness around her mouth as she pressed her lips so tightly, they were nonexistent. When she turned her hawk eyes onto me, I had to force myself not to shrink back.

"Headmaster Swordson, how good to see you." My grandfather shook hands with the headmaster before taking the seat next to me. "Max." he patted me on the hand with a grim expression.

My grandmother stared hard at me before turning her attention to the headmaster. God forbid she forget her manners. "I spoke to Headmistress McClain down at the high school. I'm sorry about your daughter."

My eyes swiveled back to the headmaster. His daughter? What was wrong with her?

"Thank you," the headmaster said softly, nodding his head. "Things have been hard."

"As always, we are here for anything you need." My grandmother's expression softened just a tiny micro-fraction before she turned her blazing glare onto me. "I thank you for arranging this meeting for us as well since my granddaughter refuses to answer my calls."

I sank into my chair tucking my chin into my chest. "I meant to call you back. I just got busy."

"Oh?" The surprise in my grandmother's voice had me lifting my head. "Busy doing what? Spreading your legs for every wizard who looks your way."

My eyes widened. So that was what this was about. I'd have been surprised that my grandmother even knew about social media, let alone was up to date on all the nasty rumors going around about me.

"So, you don't deny it?" My grandmother crossed her arms over her stomach and tapped her foot. "Do you know what this kind of scandal says about our family? How many calls I have gotten about the whole fiasco."

"Fiasco?" I scoffed, straightening up in my seat. "I'm not exactly sure what fiasco you are talking about, and I assure you, not that it's any of your business, but I haven't been spreading my legs for anyone."

My grandmother sniffed. "Well, that's a relief. Who are you dating so we can make a formal announcement and put this whole drama behind us?"

"All of them."

The headmaster made a sound between a choke and a laugh, while my grandfather hummed. My grandmother was on the verge of having a heart attack, much to my pleasure.

She breathed heavily, her hand to the lapel of her pastel green suit jacket. "What do you mean all of them? You can't be serious."

I stood, putting myself in her personal bubble. "Oh, I'm quite serious. I am dating all four of them, and we are quite happy together." Okay, so I wasn't officially dating Aidan, but she didn't know that. "Do you have a problem with that?" I placed my hands on my hips and stared her down, daring her to say something. Should have known better. We had the same genes after all.

"Of course, I do, and you certainly will not." If it had been me, I'd have stomped my foot to make my point, but I guess age taught my grandmother how to throw a fit like an adult.

"I certainly will and am." The taunting tone of my voice made me smile.

"No Mancaster will be associated with such acts of debauchery."

I snorted. "Well, it's a good thing I'm not a Mancaster."

My grandmother gasped, her eyes going wide as saucers and a hint of sadness colored her voice. "I thought we were getting somewhere, but you're just as reckless and unreasonable as your mother."

"No, I'm not." I shook my head. "I'm just not going to change who I am and what I want because you say so. I'm sorry, but I barely know you. Either of you." I turned to look at my grandfather who had sat there quietly watching us. "And you don't know me. So, I think it's better for all of us if we stopped trying to make this something it's not." I didn't wait for their answer before moving toward the door.

"Max," my grandfather called out, making me stop with a sigh. "I apologize for our assumptions, but we do just want what's best for you, even if we go about it in an unorthodox manner."

"I know, and I appreciate it, but you have to know something about me. I'm not that girl." I twisted back around, so my back was to the door. “I won’t compromise myself for someone else’s agenda, no matter their good intentions.” I shot my grandmother a look. “Headmaster.” I nodded toward him before opening the door.

This time, my grandmother stopped me. “Have you decided on a major?”

Smiling, I glanced over my shoulder at her. “Political Science in the magical world.”

“Well.” She laced her fingers in front of her and crossed over to me. “If you need a sponsor for your booth, please keep us in mind. While we might not have the same opinions on personal matters, I do think you would benefit from our influence, especially in your field of study.”

I bobbed my head. “Thank you. I will.”

Chapter 10

WHEN I LEFT THE headmaster's office, Dale was waiting for me. Paul had disappeared, but I wasn't too worried about it. He'd message me when he could.

"Hey." Dale slid an arm around my shoulders and walked me out of the office. "Are you okay?"

I nodded. "Yeah, I guess."

"Want to talk about it?"

Leaning my head against Dale's chest, I sighed. "Not really. I'm going to go to my room and crawl into bed. I just want this day to be over."

Dale made a sound in his throat that I could only translate as disapproval. I lifted my head up and stared up at him. "What?"

"I just find it funny how easily you let things get to you." Dale's hand tightened on my shoulder, his face pinching in irritation. "I mean, it's the first day of classes, and you're already skipping?"

I snorted. "I already played the tough guy act earlier. I'm all out of toughness."

"But the day is only halfway over, you're going to miss out on so much, not to mention the rumors that will start from all this." He gestured back toward the administrator's office. "By now, Sabrina has told everyone and their mom about what happened in the library and how you got called to the headmaster's. Don't forget your grandparents came and you can't say no one saw them come in."

"So?"

Dale lifted a brow at me, pausing in the hallway toward my dorm room. "So, you're just going to let them do whatever they want, even when you know it's not true?"

Lifting a shoulder and dropping it, I stared down at the ground as I shook my head. "I can't make them believe anything they don't want to. Besides, I put my time in for the day. I even have pants on." I patted my legs earning me a laugh from Dale. "But this day has bent me over and made me it's bitch. I think I've earned the right to roll over and call it a day."

Staring at me for a moment, Dale seemed to be considering my words. He seemed to have figured out something because he used his middle finger to push up his glasses and then gave me a small smile. "Well, if you're going to call it a day, I can be a supportive boyfriend and at least keep you company."

"Really?" The surprise in my voice came out before I could stop it. I cleared my throat and started back down the hall. Most of the students were in class, so we didn't have an audience for my walk of shame which had nothing to do with why I slid my hand into Dale's.

"So, you're not even going to say anything about me calling myself your boyfriend?"

"No." I pressed my lips together tightly, holding back a grin.

"So, am I?"

"Are you what?"

"Your boyfriend."

I cocked a brow and glanced over at him. "Do you want to be?"

Dale dropped my hand and tucked his hands in his pockets, his shoulders coming up to his ears as his face colored a bright red. He avoided my gaze as he muttered, "Of course, I do. I just didn't know if you ... you know wanted to."

Giggling, I grabbed Dale by the arm and pulled him the last few feet to my room. As I dug out my key and inserted it into the lock, I talked over my shoulder. "Look, I just spent the better part of a half hour defending the fact that I was dating four people to my grandmother. I'm not about to take all that back." Pushing the door open, I grinned up at Dale. "What kind of girl would that make me?"

Smiling back at me, Dale's eyes brightened with mirth. "We couldn't have that, now can we?"

Moving into the room, I dropped my bag on the desk next to my bed. Trina wasn't there, probably sitting in class right now being a good little student. Unlike me.

Letting out a huff, I went to my dresser and pulled out my favorite pair of pajamas. They were pink and grey with little donuts and coffee cups on them. I turned from the dresser, and my eyes landed on Dale standing by the still open door. "You want to close that?"

Dale's gaze went to my clothes and then the door before he quickly shut it behind him. He kept his back to me, giving me permission to change without him looking. I pulled my shirt over my head and replaced it with the grey one. As I shimmied my jeans down my legs, heat warmed in my belly. The tips of Dale's ears were red, and he fidgeted every time I moved. It was like even though he couldn't see me, the very thought of me being undressed in the same room as him was turning him on. I couldn't deny it gave me a little thrill as well.

"I'm done," I told him after I pulled my pajama pants on and moved over to the bed. I propped my pillows up and sat down, leaning against them.

Dale stood there staring at me, unsure of what to do.

I patted the seat next to me and gave him a flirty grin. "Come here. You can't keep me company from all the way over there."

Clearing his throat, Dale slipped his shoes off before climbing into the bed with me. His arm brushed mine as we settled in together. I might have seemed all confident asking him to come over here, but now that he was in the bed with me, I was all nerves. I hadn't been in a bed with a guy since Jaron, and that turned out *oh* so well.

"So," I clucked my tongue, "want to watch a movie?"

Dale stared at my room, his brow furrowed. "How are we going to do that?"

I reached over his legs, grabbing for my laptop. I had to reach to get to it, my fingers barely getting a hold of it as I stretched my arm beyond its capacity.

"Want me to get that for you?" Dale's voice next to my ear strained.

"I've almost got it." I winced and then grinned when I pulled the laptop into my hands. I sat up and came face to face with Dale. His breath felt hot against my cheek, his eyes darkened over, and a sort of pained expression covered his face. Still thrown over his lap, I could easily feel the hardness pressed against my side.

The laptop sat between us in my hands, but I was suddenly not thinking about watching a movie anymore. Licking my lips, I ducked my head, but Dale stopped me with a finger to my chin. With one hand, he took my laptop and sat it back on the nightstand while his other cupped my face. My hands rested on his chest, where my fingers curled into the fabric of his shirt. Leaning forward so that our breath mingled, my eyelids fluttered. Our lips brushed against each other at the same time my breasts skimmed his chest, making my nipples tighten deliciously.

"I'm going to kiss you." Dale's husky voice rumbled through me, setting my blood on fire.

Swallowing thickly, I blinked up at him. "I thought that was what we were doing."

The edge of his lip curled up. "If you don't know when I'm kissing you, then I'm doing something wrong."

I breathed heavily. "Believe me. You're not doing anything wrong."

"Well, I better make sure it sticks." He chuckled for a moment before his mouth came down on to mine. His fingers tangled into my hair, pulling me closer to him until I was on his lap in an awkward angle. Not really knowing what I was doing, I shifted until my legs straddled him, pressing our cores against one another. A strangled sound came from Dale. His hands dropped down to my waist and then, after a thought, to my hips. I didn't give him the time to ask for permission before I ground my center against him, making us both groan.

His tongue lapped at mine, my hands cupping his face to pull him even closer. The world tipped sideways, and I was on my back, Dale hovering above me. Breathing heavily, my legs fell to either side, and Dale sat between them, almost afraid to come too close. I couldn't have that. Pulling his face back down to mine, I wrapped my legs around his waist, jerking his hips to mine.

A grunt bumped from Dale as our teeth clashed together. Sliding my tongue along his lower lip, I nipped at it pulling it between my teeth. Dale's hand clapped down on the bed next to my head, the hand on my hip urged my hips upward as he pressed against me. A delicious friction began in my center, and a groan slipped from my lip as I gasped. Dale pushed up my shirt, the warm pads of his fingers tickling my sides.

I giggled, pulling away from his tempting mouth.

"I'm not sure laughing is what I'm going for," Dale breathed with a huff, his eyes twinkling with amusement and arousal.

"Sorry." I chewed on my lower lip and stared up at him.

Dale's hand moved further up beneath my shirt, making my breath hitch. "Just don't do it again." I didn't have a chance to respond before his mouth was on mine once more. I only half participated, my attention focused mostly on the hand still inching up to my skin. When his hand curved over my bra-clad chest, I gave up kissing him back all together.

Eyes locking with mine, Dale's tongue dipped out and licked his lower lip. He fumbled for the clip to my bra, and I reached back underneath my shirt and unsnapped it. Pulling my arms into my shirt, I drew my arms out of the straps and whipped it out through my sleeve hole. Grinning up at Dale's surprised expression, I only had a second to gloat before my breath hitched. Neither of us was grinning when Dale's hand touched my bare skin, kneaded at the flesh of my breasts and plucking at the tips. I arched into his hand, wetness pooling between my thighs as our bodies lined up.

"Max," Dale drew out, his voice low and scratchy. "I want to see you."

Mouth dry but eager to have him see me as well, I sat up. Dale moved back as I grabbed the bottom of my shirt and pulled it over my head, baring my skin to the air and Dale's scorching gaze. Not wanting to be the only one unclothed, I reached up to the buttons of Dale's shirt. He didn't stop me as I slowly undid each button. I pressed my lips to the muscled skin that became visible, placing open mouth kisses to his flesh. When I reached the end of the line, my finger dipped into the top of his pants, making him gasp.

"Not yet," Dale grabbed my hand in his and placed it on his chest. He leaned down as if to kiss me but bypassed my face and moved to my neck. The hot press of his mouth and tongue against the junction of my neck and shoulder had me angling my head to the side. That same burning heat moved down my collarbone and continued down until he had me gasping.

I held onto Dale's hair, holding him to me as his lips curled around my nipple. He tugged and skimmed his teeth against the sensitive tip, making my hips buck involuntarily. The ball of light in my mind's eyes grew brighter as Dale's mouth moved from one breast to the other, his hand dropping to the waistband of my pants.

"Uh, wait." I gasped and licked my lips, panic starting to rise inside of me. Dale must not have heard me because his mouth followed his hand, trailing along my belly button to my pubic bone. I tugged on his hair forcing his head up. "Wait a second. I can't ... I can't breathe."

Dale peered up at me, and the hunger in his expression almost had me regretting stopping him. However, I didn't like the feeling inside of me. It wasn't like when I'd had my first time with Jaron. We made out and even fooled around several times before we ever got together, but none of those times did my magic flare up like this. I didn't trust myself or my magic to behave.

"Are you okay?" Dale asked, moving back from me giving me room to breathe.

I shook my head and sat up. "No, I mean, I don't know. My skin feels tight, kind of buzzing, and my magic ... it's—"

"Okay, Max."

My head jerked up to meet his calm expression. "I've had this feeling before and that was usually right before I set someone on fire or worse. I don't know about you, but I'd not like our first time together to end with burning down the school."

Dale chuckled and then brushed my hair away from my face. "Don't worry, it happens to everyone their first time. You just have to trust yourself to stay in control."

"But I'm not in control." I pushed him away and grabbed my shirt, pulling it over my head. "It's not that I don't want to." I huffed a laugh. "Believe me everything inside of me is screaming yes, yes." Dale smirked. "But I also like you and, like you said, I need to trust myself, but I don't." I shook my head and sucked in several lungfuls of air. "Not yet."

"That's fine, Max." Dale cupped my face and turned me to meet his gaze. "I'm not going to push you before you're ready. I just want you to know, you can trust me. I won't let anything bad happen."

Clutching his hand with mine, I leaned into his touch and closed my eyes briefly. When I opened my mouth to tell him how much that meant to me, I was interrupted by the door opening. Crap, the lock.

"Uh, hey." Trina held the door half open and then quickly shut it at the sight of Dale's bare chest. "Am I interrupting something?"

"No."

"Yes."

I shot a look at Dale. "No, you're fine. What are you doing here?"

Trina moved over to her desk and grabbed a book, holding it up. "I forgot my Potions book. You not going to class?"

I shook my head. "No. Too much drama today."

Trina's nose wrinkled. "Yeah, I heard. Sorry about that, but did you really make Sabrina hit someone?"

My elbow on my knee, I laughed and facepalmed. "Yes, but that wasn't my intention."

"Either way, that's awesome." Trina giggled, and then her eyes trailed over to a quiet Dale. "You here to brighten her day?"

Blushing, I moved to the edge of the bed so that I covered most of Dale's naked chest. "He's just leaving."

"I am?" Dale asked, his voice hot against my ear.

I grabbed his shirt and tossed it at him. "Yes, you are." I ushered him to the door, while he still buttoned his shirt up. Kissing him on the lips, I gave him a little shove and wave. "I'll text you."

Trina grinned and tossed her bag down. "So, that's an interesting development."

Blushing to my roots, I collapsed onto my bed. "Don't you have class to get to?"

Chapter 11

"ARE YOU GOING TO ask her?" I shoved a French fry into my mouth and pointed another one at Trina. "Valentine's day is next week."

Trina stuck her fork in the salad on her plate, not taking a bite as she scowled. "I don't know. Libby and I haven't gotten past the flirting stage yet. I'm not sure we're ready for a Valentine's Day date." She glanced over toward the table that held her current crush, Libby Moreling. Libby sat snuggly between her best friends, Monica Magenski and Sabrina Craftsman. While Sabrina might be a complete horror, Monica had proven to be pretty nice, Libby too though she wasn't very bright.

"What happened?" I swirled my French fry in some ketchup. "I thought you were going to ask her out at Halloween?"

"No." Shoulders sagging, Trina picked up a cherry tomato and popped it into her mouth. She looked like a chipmunk with the tomato sitting in her cheek, and she bit down onto it with an annoyed expression, like it was the tomato's fault she chickened out.

"Why not?"

Her lips twisted into a grimace, she muttered, "Not the right moment."

"What, the aftermath of Sabrina's meltdown not romantic enough?" I sniffed, cracking a smile. "I would think that would be the perfect moment. You would have become her knight, or rather witch, in shining armor."

"Yeah, right. She was too worried about Sabrina getting hurt to pay me any mind." She stabbed at the lettuce on her plate, grumbling under her breath and shooting pitiful looks in Libby's direction.

I hated to see her like this. Trina was great and attractive too – you know for a female. Boobs weren't really my thing. She was the best roommate I'd ever had. Always good for a late-night snack run. If that wasn't a good trait for a girlfriend, I didn't know what was?

"Well, it's her loss, but I still think you should ask." I saw Aidan out of the corner of my eye, and half stood to wave him over. To Trina, I said, "You never know."

"Hello." Aidan nodded to Trina and then sat beside me, his bulky form forcing his arms to brush against me. A pleasant tingle formed where our skin touched, but I pushed it off.

"Get a vision of me craving fries?" I smirked at him waving a fry in his face.

Aidan's eyes narrowed. “I do eat.”

Flushing at his intense gaze, I stared down at my plate. “Oh. Sorry.”

“However, I did glimpse ahead to make sure you would be here.”

Looking up from my plate, I crinkled my nose at his self-satisfied grin – a mere twitch of the lips really – before launching a fry at his face. Of course, Aidan opened his mouth and caught the fry, chewing it with a smirk.

“So, did you want something, or did you just want to make googly eyes at my girl?” Trina mocked, something that few people would dare.

Aidan didn't bother to answer her before getting up and heading to the cafeteria line.

“Well, isn't he delightful?” Trina mused, shoving a forkful of salad into her mouth. In between chewing, she pointed her fork at me. “You know if you're going to start collecting strays you could at least get some with some real talents.”

“I'm not collecting strays,” I scoffed at her crossing my arms over my chest. “And besides, plenty of them have great skills.”

Trina arched a dark brow. “Like what, besides having hot bods? You can't spend all day getting your freak on. Not that I'm against sexathons, but come on, there's got to be more to a relationship.”

I sputtered in my drink and glared at her. “I'm not having a sexathon. I haven't done it with any of them yet.”

“Really? That's really too bad. If people were going to talk shit about me, I’d at least want some of that shit to be true. You know, the good parts.” She wiggled her brows at me suggestively and frowned. “But for not even one part of it to be true? That's just sad.”

I snorted. “Well, if someone hadn't interrupted us, I'd have at least gotten—"

“Gotten what?”

I choked on my words and blushed red at Aidan's question. I didn't even hear him return. How a guy that big could be that quiet took some mad skills.

“Gotten a good grade on that assignment,” I quickly spat out and then started to Trina for confirmation who looked way too amused. “Isn't that right?”

Trina nodded, her afro bobbing with the movement. “Oh yeah, Max is all about getting it good.”

Glowering at my now ex-friend, I stood up. “I hate to cut this short, but I have class.” To Aidan, I offered a small smile. “Catch you next time?”

With a wink that surprised me, Aidan said, “I'll be seeing you.”

Shaking my head as I chortled, I made my way out of the cafeteria and headed toward my next class. Potions.

So far, the class hadn't been too bad. I was far from a master at it, but I hadn't blown anyone up yet. Today, however, we were choosing our projects for our final exam. There was a mixture of different ones I could end up getting, all of which could be difficult on their own out of a classroom setting.

Ones I'd heard could be assigned were things like the draught of death. It could put its drinker into a death-like sleep, but Lady's Luck was what I hoped to get. Not only because it had a short ingredient list but because I could use a bit of luck on my side. Unfortunately, it was one of the harder ones to brew.

Many of the females in the class wanted things like a love potion, which really wasn't real love but obsession or lust. I so didn't need any more of that in my life. I had a hard enough time juggling the ones I had.

When I arrived at the classroom, I was happy to see I was one of the first ones there. Our professor, Alice Bromwick, nodded at me in greeting before going back to whatever she was working on at her station. As far as teachers went, she was nice, if a bit odd, way better than last semester's professor. At least,

Professor Bromwick kept her feet on the ground when she taught.

I sat my bag on the table I'd taken to sit at. The table was not quite so far up front that I had the professor's attention but not so far back that I seemed like a slacker. A happy middle ground. Somewhere I hoped I'd find between my witch and human life.

My magical life, whether I wanted it to or not, seemed to have taken over the majority of my time. I rarely could do any normal human girl things anymore. Everything was magic this and spells that, and don't make friends with humans or they'll find out!

Little late for that.

As if knowing I was thinking of her, my phone buzzed.

Callie: Man, can this class get any lamer. Business 101 what a snooze fest.

Me: LOL. I feel ya.

Callie: What fun magical things are you doing? Any wand measuring?

I blushed at Callie's question and started to type out a reply when my phone was ripped out of my hands.

"Oh, what have we here?" Sabrina held my phone up high as she walked back to the last table where she and Monica usually sat.

"Give it back, Sabrina," I bit out, my hand going to the necklace.

"Or what? You'll sic me on another student?" she sneered.

At the reminder of what happened last time I made a wish, I released the necklace. I started to think of some argument or comeback, but before I could let it out, my phone floated out of Sabrina's hands and back into mine.

"Now, that's enough of that. Unless you'd like me to make this a partnered assignment?" Sabrina and I gaped at Professor Bromwick before shaking our heads. "Good, then I suggest you take your seats, so we can begin."

Sabrina shot me the evil eye but went to her seat. Monica, who had already taken hers, gave me a small wave when Sabrina wasn't looking. Why she was still friends with her was a mystery to me. Sabrina was the ultimate mean girl. She'd say nice things to your face and nasty ones behind your back. Sometimes she wasn't even that nice and would just say the mean crap to your face.

I had learned from Monica that she not only terrorized everyone around her but her friends as well. When Monica wanted to major in Potions, she was told she couldn't because Paul, Sabrina's ex, was majoring in Potions. A shit reason to kill someone's dreams but then again Monica let her do it. I couldn't help stupid.

"So, as you all know today, we will decide on your class project." Professor Bromwick stood at the head of the class, her hands behind her back. Her eagle-like eyes scanned the room for anyone not paying attention, not that anyone would dare. No one wanted to repeat her class.

The classroom door opened loudly, and everyone's eyes turned to it. Trina froze in the doorway and then ducked her head in shame as she hurried over to take the seat next to me.

"What'd I miss?" she whispered.

"Just Sabrina's bs."

Professor Bromwick cleared her throat, and Trina and I clammed up with equal looks of contrition on our faces.

"This assignment counts for sixty percent of your overall grade, so it is safe to say if you mess this up there's no helping you." Professor Bromwick's gaze scanned the room.

A guy in the front raised his hand with a doofus grin on his face.

"Yes?"

"So, what you're saying is we can pretty much ignore all the homework and only do this assignment and still pass?" All eyes turned from the guy to Professor Bromwick.

Trina stifled a giggle next to me.

Sighing with clear disdain, the professor fluffed the collar of her maroon button-down shirt before answering. "Yes. You could say that."

"Awesome." The guy in front grinned and slapped hand with his buddies.

"However," the sharp tone to Professor Bromwick's voice pulled all of our attention, "anyone who thinks they can go through life with a half-ass understanding of potions is a walking accident waiting to happen." Her eyes zeroed in on the guy in front who had stopped laughing. "I would think hard on skipping the coursework altogether if you value your limbs."

The guy nodded and swallowed visibly, his friends no longer laughing either. Some people.

"We will be choosing your assignment in the fairest way possible, and to make sure there are no repeats and no chances of copying someone else's work, I have selected the potions." The papers she had been working on at her desk floated into the air. They ripped themselves into halves and then further down to fourths and then eighths, so there were more than enough papers for each of the fifteen students in our class.

Professor Bromwick picked up a bowl from her table, and the papers promptly flew into it. Holding the bowl up high, she walked by each student, allowing them to take only one. The expressions on the student's faces as they saw their assignment either said they were going to pass or fail this one.

My leg jiggled as I waited for my turn. Trina chewed on her thumbnail, her eyes following our professor around the room. Sabrina squealed with delight, making me jump and whip around to see her. A smug expression covered her face as she settled in her seat. Soon enough it was our turn.

Trina was first. She reached a shaky hand into the bowl and scrambled for a slip. Pulling it out, she unfolded it and sagged with relief in her seat.

Good news, it looked like.

My turn.

Holding my breath, I reached into the bowl and grabbed ahold of one of the ripped-up papers. Pulling it out of the bowl, I brought it down in front of me. I started down at the folded paper not daring to open it yet. My fingers brushed against my necklace as I wished with all my might to get a good one.

“Guardian Light?” I must have been mistaken. This couldn’t be my assignment. This was like Advanced Potions. Not easy at all.

“Oh, man. That blows.” Trina gave me a side hug.

The person in front of me turned in their seat and snorted. “Sucks to be you.”

“Hey, mind your own business.” Trina snapped at them, then turned to me. “Don't listen to them.”

Sighing again, I stared down at my slip of paper. I'd wished for a good assignment. Was the necklace broken?

“As well as making the potion, you will also be required to write a five-page essay about the uses and precautions of it," Professor Bromwick went on to say as if she didn't realize she had given me something a first year would not know how to do. I stared at my paper until she had dismissed class and approached my table. "Miss Norman? Class has dismissed. Did you have a question?"

Licking my lips, I held up my paper.

She took it from me and read over it before handing it back to me. "Guardian Light?" Even her eyes widened in surprise. "I do not remember placing such a potion in the bowl."

My head jerked up. "You didn't?"

Lips pressed together tightly, she quipped, "No, but these things are not unheard of. Magic had a way of doing what it wants. Clearly, it feels you would benefit from such a potion." She tossed the paper back to me where I fluttered down to the tabletop. "The Guardian Light potion creates, for lack of a better word, a sort of guardian angel. It'll give you warning when you are in danger and, when created properly, can last for several years. It's a pretty complicated spell with the ability to give you a great advantage. I suggest you not screw it up."

With those words of encouragement, she stalked back to the front of the room. Well, no one ever said this school would be easy.

Chapter 12

TAPPING MY PEN AGAINST my notebook and my leg jiggling beneath the desk in my room, I sighed.

Besides dealing with grade changing projects, I also had the booth for the spring fair. I had no idea how I was going to pull that off. I'd never made a booth before, let alone one for political science.

Sighing again, I laid my head on top of my notebook.

"Well, that sounds like you've made great progress." Trina closed the door behind her. She stood next to me, drying her face and neck off with a towel.

"I know." I stuck my tongue out at my blank page.

"I thought you were sure you'd figure something out before I got back from my run."

Yeah, I know. Trina was one of those people, the 'I love to run for fun' kind of people. She was lucky that she was my roommate, or I'd have never talked to her.

"Yeah, well, I lied."

Trina tapped her chin in thought and then a devilish grin curled up her face. "You know who you should ask for help?"

I stared at her suspiciously and then asked, "Who?"

"Well, who do you know that has an exclusive insight into the magical world of politics?"

I winced and raised a brow. "My grandmother?"

Trina made a face. "No way. After the stunt she pulled? I wouldn't suggest asking her if she was the last person on earth." When I still didn't know what she was talking about, she shook the back of my chair with vigor. "Hello? The Broomsteins! Your boy toys are from one of the major magical families in the whole state!"

"Pfft." I pushed her away from my chair. "One, they are *not* my boy toys."

"Yeah, okay." Trina rolled her eyes.

"Two, I'm not sure they'd appreciate me using them for my school work."

Trina winked and parroted back my words from the other day. "Can't hurt to ask."

Pursing my lips together, I scowled. Then I had an idea. Grinning, I picked up my phone and pointed it at Trina. “I'll ask them to help if you ask Libby out.”

Trina crossed her arms and pouted. “You don't fight fair.”

“Well,” I picked up my amulet and held it up, “I could always use one of my wishes.” Trina gasped and darted toward me, reaching for the necklace.

“Don't you dare!”

Laughing and holding it out of her reach, I exclaimed, “It's for your own good. I’m just thinking of your future.” I rushed away from her to stand on the bed with Trina hot on my heels.

“Well, I can tell you what's not in my future,” Trina growled, her hands up poised and ready to attack. “A blonde-haired witch.”

“Oh yeah?” I countered, jumping from side to side. “And why's that?”

“Because I’m going to tickle her to death!” She launched herself at me, knocking me on my back and the air whooshed out of me. Then it was a fight for dominance. Trina's fingers found my sides, and I struggled to breathe through my laughter, all while holding onto the necklace.

“Do you give up?”

“Never!” I shouted at her through chuckles. A throat clearing interrupted our fight, and we both sat up.

Ian stood in our doorway his hands tucked in his pockets, a mischievous glint in his eyes. I shoved Trina off me, quickly adjusting my hair out of my face which was quickly turning red from pure mortification.

"I knocked but then I heard the yelling and thought someone might need help, but I can see I overreacted." He grinned so broadly my heart skipped a beat.

"Why, look who it is?" Trina gave me a sly grin before sliding off the bed and walking toward Ian. "We were just talking about you."

Crossing his arms over his chest, Ian smirked. "All good, I hope?"

"Of course!" I rushed to answer, jumping to my feet before Trina could say otherwise. Twisting my hands behind my back, I shyly glanced up at Ian. "I'm surprised to see you. You haven't been around lately." I tucked my hair behind my ear and dipped my eyes down to the ground. "I thought maybe you saw the—"

"The craziness Sabrina started?" Ian offered, coming closer to me. His fingers tipped my chin up to meet his swirling brown and green eyes.

"Yeah," I breathed, the room suddenly feeling stifling.

"It'll take a lot more than that to get rid of me." Ian leaned forward and brushed his lips against mine, sending a thrilling zing down my body and out my toes.

“Wow, is it hot in here or just me?” Trina announced, waving her hand at her face.

Flushing brightly, I stepped away from Ian and his tempting lips. If Ian was bothered, he didn’t show it.

Trina shifted from side to side and then turned and grabbed her toiletry bag. “Well, I'm going to go grab a shower then head to the library. I have an essay on the uses of dried newt versus fresh due on Monday.” Grinning, she headed for the door. Before she left, she winked. “Don't do anything I wouldn’t do!”

Alone with Ian, I didn't know what to do. Well, I knew what my body wanted to do, but like I’d told Dale, I wasn't so sure that was a good idea.

“So, you wanted to talk to me about something?” I shifted away from Ian's intense gaze to where my blank notebook sat.

I could feel him moving behind me, and I forced myself to relax and not show how much being alone with him affected me.

“Can't I just come by to see you?” His breath brushed along the back of my neck making me regret the ponytail I’d put my hair in. His hands slid around my waist and drew me against him.

My heart raced at his nearness, and I gulped. “Sure, you can. I needed to talk to you anyway.” I grabbed my notebook and shifted around, pushing it into his face. "I need ideas for my booth."

"Booth?"

"Yeah I'm entering the contest at the Spring Fair. I have to make a booth depicting my major." I lifted a shoulder before dropping it with a disgruntled sigh.

"What's your major?"

"Political science."

Ian frowned. "Not that I don't want to help you, but why don't you ask your grandparents for help?"

I quirked a brow at him. "This coming from the guy who doesn't even talk to his own parents?"

Ian tilted his head back and sighed. "Understandable. So, what do you need me to do?"

Moving out from under his arms, I sat down on the edge of the bed. "Really, I just don't know where to start. I had plans for when I was going to go to Brown, but I don't know much about magical politics." I grinned at him. "Do you guys have a bunch of old people sitting around a cauldron, discussing the economic impact of toadstools in the day to day market?"

"I can explain the basics of our political system, but I don't know much about the economic effects of toadstool sales." Ian's lips ticked up at the sides, and then he snapped his fingers. "You know who would be great to ask? Paul. He's the one our parents are grooming to take over, not me." I didn't miss the slight bitterness in his tone, but I didn't address it.

Before I could comment one way or the other, he whipped out his phone and put it to his ear. "Hey. You busy? ... Good. Come to Max's." Hanging up, Ian explained, "He'll be here in two minutes."

"Who?"

"Paul, of course."

I gaped at him. Both of them here? In the same room with me. That sounded like a bad idea waiting to happen. Not only because of the tension still going on between the two of them, but because I wasn't sure I could have that much hotness in one room.

What are you gonna do when all your guys want to hang out together?

I shoved that nagging thought away. I hadn't really thought that far ahead. Here I was, enjoying my time with all of them individually, but I never really stopped to think what it would be like to have them all in one room. Were any of them even friends?

"How do you know Dale?" I asked, curiously. They had acknowledged each other on my first day of school, but it hadn't necessarily been a good interaction.

Ian lifted a shoulder. "Most of us around here pretty much grew up together. Went to the same elementary and everything." He started opening one of my drawers and lifted a pair of my sexier underwear out.

"Stop that." I snatched it from his hand with a scowl. "But I thought Dale was a more normal wizard?" Ian gave me a strange look, so I quickly added, "I mean, you know, not magical royalty or whatever." I waved a hand in his direction.

Ian snorted. "Honestly, you're more royalty than any of us, not that you'd know it with your scandalous ways." He tugged on my ponytail with a mischievous grin.

Jerking my ponytail of his hands, I jabbed a finger at his chest. "I don't see you complaining considering you're part of that scandal."

Ian wrapped his hands around my waist, pulling me toward him. "And you won't because I don't mind sharing." He dipped his head down and captured my mouth in a searing kiss.

I broke the kiss before it could go much further. "Not as long as you get an equal share, right?"

"Right."

"Knock, knock." Our heads turned in unison to where Paul stood in the doorway. His expression was cautious as if he wasn't certain if he was wanted.

Releasing Ian, I went to the door. Opening it further, I ushered Paul inside. "Hey, you got here fast."

Paul stared at Ian for a moment, before turning to give me one of his knee buckling smiles. "Yeah, I was heading this way anyway."

I could feel the tension in the room. None of us knew how to react to all three in one space, just like I had worried. Eager to break the tension, I acted as if it were no big deal as I popped up and kissed Paul before taking a seat at my desk.

"So, what was the big hurry for?" Paul asked, taking my lead and asking as if it were all normal.

"Max needs help with her booth for the fair," Ian explained, leaning against Trina's desk.

"Why me, though?"

Ian locked eyes with me, grinning like a fool. "Max has decided to take on the big bad world of magical politics."

"I see." Paul stroked his jaw before turning to me. "Well, what do you know about our society so far?"

I shrugged. "You have some council that regulates the use of magic and what humans know about it. Things like that."

"That's it?"

"I mean, I took History of Magic, and I'm taking Etiquette of Magic now. What more really is there?" I straddled my chair so I could see them both, leaning my face on the back.

Paul's voice filled with excitement as he took a seat on my bed near me. "That's just the tip of it. You really have to cram yourself all the way in to get the depth of it all."

I tried to hold back my laughter at his analogy, but one look at Ian and I couldn't hold it anymore. As Ian and I laughed, Paul just stared at us in confusion.

"What? What did I say?"

Not answering Paul, I asked Ian, "Does he do this often?"

"More often than you'd think." Ian shook his head. "How he ended up the heir, I'll never know."

That comment caused the laughter to die and the tension to return. Paul stared down at the ground his voice low. "I never asked for it, you know."

My eyes jerked to Ian who seemed to regret his words.

"I know. I didn't mean to imply—"

"I know," Paul interrupted him, standing from the bed. "It's fine." I could see where this was going, and I fought to find a way to stop them from storming out of here in a huff.

"You know what I wish?" I hopped out of my seat and placed myself between the two of them. They watched me expectantly, and I grinned coyly. "I wish you'd ask me out for

Valentine's." The necklace in my pocket warmed, signaling it had heard my request.

Immediately, Ian and Paul asked at the same time, "Will you be my date for Valentine's?"

While they tried to figure out what had just happened, I kissed them each on the lips before skipping toward the door. "I'd love to."

"Hey, I see what you did there." Paul pointed an accusatory finger at me but smiled none the less.

"Too late. You already agreed." I giggled and winked as I darted out the door.

Chapter 13

"SO, LET ME GET this straight. The Magical Council called the Watchers monitor all of the magic in the world, and they put the smack down on those abusing their powers or threatening to expose us?" I read from the paper in front of me and then looked up at Paul who sat across from me in the library.

Ian had to go do something mysterious in the basement level, so it left Paul to help me with the booth. We'd been going over the structure of the magical community for well over an hour, and I was ready to put a wand through my ear, into my brain, and wiggle it around a bit. Maybe then it would make sense.

"Not quite." Paul winced. "The Watchers only monitor this area. There are different factions for each district."

"And how many districts are there again?" I held my pen poised and ready to scribble down what he said.

"In the US? Thirteen, but that's counting the ones who cover Alaska and Hawaii. Alaska's usually lumped in with Canada and Hawaii with Mexico." He drew a picture of the district set up on my notepad, circling clusters of states as he explained.

"Why is Texas by itself?"

Paul grinned. "Because everything is bigger in Texas and that means the attitudes. Plus, most of the people are spread out, not to forget about the fairy colonies that take up a good part of it. They kind of need all the regulation they can get."

"Fairy colonies? Hold up now." I slammed my hands down on the table and leaned over it. "You're saying fairies exist, and you are only telling me this now?"

Paul chuckled at my reaction. He reached up and tweaked my nose, making me scowl and sit back down my hand rubbing my nose. "If I had known you were so interested in mythical beings, I'd have mentioned it before. Most of us learned about them growing up." He shrugged an apologetic smile. "I guess we just assumed you knew."

Letting out an aggravated growl, I leaned back in my chair with my arms tight over my chest. "From now on let's just all assume Max knows nothing. Just call me John Snow and get it over with."

Throwing his head back, Paul laughed loud enough we got shushed by the librarian. I couldn't bother to feel contrite with how gorgeous he sounded doing it. I mean, give a girl some warning or at least a fresh pair of underwear afterward.

"Okay so ..." I cleared my throat and shifted in my seat, my thighs pressing together to subdue the throbbing there. "You think I should make the focus of my booth combining human and magical life together?"

"Yes." Paul nodded, moving closer to the table. "You have been saying how you didn't know anything about our world until last year and now you're playing catchup. I mean, we have a twelve-year advantage on you. How do they expect you to catch up so fast?"

The way he said it made me depressed. How was I going to have any chance of catching up? Yeah, I had a good amount of powers, but no knowledge behind them. "It's like I need some kind of spell to catch me up," I muttered to myself.

"What was that?" Paul angled his head toward me.

I growled in annoyance. "I was just thinking how right you were. There's no chance for us human-raised witches. There needs to be some kind of spell or something to catch us up with you all."

"That's a great idea! You should make your booth about that." He pushed his chair back and came around the table, kneeling next to me. "You can make it your platform. The magical community is doing a disservice to those coming in late--"

"By no fault of their own," I pointed out as he scribbled on my notepad.

Paul nodded vigorously. "And explain the pros of having such a spell. Obviously, they'd have to regulate it somehow, giving it only to those who need it, or everyone would use it."

I sniffed. "Can't have that, now, can we?" I could just imagine all the kids who would clamor to skip out on the school portion to learn it all at once. It was a lot of information to absorb, which meant a lot of years of schools missed.

"Well, I think you're set now." Paul placed his hand on my chair, his fingers brushing my skin as he stood. "Now all you need is a sponsor."

I groaned and laid my head back against my chair. "Any chance your parents are charitable and looking to get in good with my family?"

Chuckling, Paul bent over and pressed his lips to my forehead, causing my eyes to flutter closed. "As much as they would be delighted to help out, I have a feeling, in this case, they would be gaining an enemy rather than a friend."

I stuck my tongue out at him, but he was right. My grandfather might not care, but my grandmother who had already offered would be pissed to find out I went somewhere else.

"Are you leaving?" I caught his hand as he moved away.

Amusement covered his face as he leaned his hip against the table. "I was thinking of going to get some of my own work done. I have a ton of papers to grade."

Wrinkling my nose, I leaned into him. "Isn't that the teacher's job?"

"Yes, and I'm the *teacher's* aide." Paul smiled down at me, pulling on my hand until I came out of my chair. He shifted us, so I stood between his thighs, his hands resting low on my hips.

"Still, I would think they would at least grade our stuff. I put so much effort into making sure there is just enough error to hide the fact that most of it came from Wikipedia. I feel like it's all gone to waste on an *assistant.*"

Paul chuckled darkly, his fingers slipping down past my hips to settle on my butt. "If you're getting your answers from the internet, we have a much larger problem than cheating." He arched up to grab my lip between his teeth, urging me down to kiss him.

Our tongues barely had a chance to taste one another before an unseen force shoved us apart. Startled by the interruption, I searched around to see the librarian with an annoyed glare.

"No fraternizing in the library."

"Sorry," I grumbled and turned to my bag. Paul lingered by my side as I gathered my things. Pulling my bag over my shoulder, I turned to him. "I better get out of here before another rumor gets spread."

Paul took my bag from me and slung it over his shoulder. "Meh, what's a life without a bit of drama?"

"Especially if that one happens to do with you, huh?" I bumped my shoulder with his as we strolled out of the library.

"I'm not the jealous type, but there's not a picture of us circulating around."

"And there isn't one with Aidan either," I reminded him.

"But there's one of you and Ian." The pout to his tone made me laugh.

"Alright, the next time the vultures descend, I'll make sure to dry hump you for the masses."

Paul stopped us at my door, pressing me up against it. "How about just for kicks?"

Swallowing thickly, I nodded dumbly. "I think that would be okay."

However, once again before his mouth could touch mine, the door behind me opened. My world tipped over, and Paul came with me. At the last minute, his hands came out to stop himself on either side of me, keeping him from crushing me.

A dark shadow hung over us, and I angled my head to see around Paul, revealing a beaming Ian. “Seems like I got back just in time.”

Paul muttered something under his breath that sounded like ‘damn cockblocker’ before inching to his feet. He offered me a hand which I gladly took.

“How'd the lesson go?” Ian asked all nonchalant-like as if he hadn’t just interrupted something.

“Well enough, until we got kicked out of the library for making out.” I grinned mischievously at Paul before another person cleared their throat. Spinning around to face the room, I scowled at Trina sitting on her bed by Aidan. “So that’s how you got in. And do I need to ask why you’re here? What did you see this time?”

Aidan didn’t answer, his eyes sparkling with laughter.

“About that.” Trina slipped off her bed and waved a finger at me. “I am not your secretary or pimp so keep up with your harem, or I’ll lock them out next time.”

“Harem?” I sputtered and blushed. “Who said anything about a harem?”

Trina turned in a circle and counted. “I count three guys, and that's not even including

Dale. That's the start of a harem if I ever saw one. In any case," Trina fluffed her hair with a sniff, "I have a date."

"With Libby?" I clapped my hands together and grinned.

"Wouldn't you like to know?" Trina pursed her lips and winked. "Don't screw on my bed. I'll know." She pointed her finger as she scanned the guys in the room before ending on me with a sing-song voice. "Have fun."

Alone in my room with three guys? Okay, this isn't too bad. I haven't slept with any of them yet. Haven't even kissed Aidan yet but the hooded expression on his face made me think that might be happening pretty soon.

"As much fun as this situation is," Paul waved a hand in front of him, "I do have work to do. So, I'm going to go."

"Okay," I said as he angled toward me to give me a chaste kiss. "I'll talk to you later and thanks again."

"No problem." His eyes went to Ian and Aidan, and he nodded. "See ya."

After he left, I started to close the door but hesitated, not sure if I wanted to put myself in that position. A warm body pressed against the length of my back, breath brushing along my neck.

"Close the door, Max." The husky tone of Ian's voice sent a shudder down my back and settled low.

I knew what I did next would be a defining moment in our relationship, not only for Ian and me but for Aidan as well. Was I ready to move forward with them? Did I want to?

"Max?" Aidan called out my name softly. "Nothing bad will happen if you say no or if you say yes."

I didn't know how much I needed reassurance at least from one of them. I needed to know that I wasn't going to ruin everything by not being ready. Several parts of me were very ready, but I was afraid. The same way I'd been afraid with Dale. Aidan's powers of foresight helped calm those fears.

Taking a deep breath, I pushed the door closed the last few inches, closing it with a resounding snap.

Mouth dry, I licked my lips and slowly turned around. Ian stood inches from me, his eyes dark with the promise of what was to come.

"So," I blinked up at him and then over to Aidan, "what's going on?"

Ian's chest rumbled, reverberating against me. Repressing a moan, I slipped away from him before he could answer.

I needed space. Everything was happening so suddenly.

"Relax," Ian commanded but didn't come after me. "We're not here to jump you."

I laughed nervously. "Could have fooled me. How do you know each other anyway?" I tried to steer the conversation away from the big, lingerie-covered elephant in the room. It was doing its best to sashay and give us a peep show, but I was the good girl in the corner who needed a few before I could get into that.

"High school," Aidan said in his usual one-word (well, two in this case) answer.

Seeing as I wasn't going to get much more from him, I turned my attention to Ian. Ian shrugged. "What he said. Aidan's actually one of my best friends."

Brows furrowed in agitation, I smacked my lips. "And you are telling me this now?"

"Would it have mattered?" Ian angled his head to the side, studying me.

"Well..." I crossed my arms over my chest and then dropped them with a sigh. "No. It wouldn't have."

Aidan stood from Trina's bed and slowly approached me as if I were a gazelle he didn't want to spook. "I have seen us together."

"That's not creepy at all." I pointed a finger at him, backing away from his approaching figure. My back bumped up against Ian, and my eyes darted around, feeling very much like the gazelle facing down a lion.

"Max." Ian brushed his hand along my arm, his voice soft in my ear. "You're fighting something you already know you want."

As he spoke the words, I knew it was true. If I really didn't want Aidan around, I could have sent him away at any time, but I let him hang around. Sure, I found him attractive and found a certain kind of calm in his quiet shadow. I sure didn't fear anyone messing with me with Aidan at my side.

Wetting my lips, I nodded slightly.

Aidan took that as the go-ahead.

"Hold on," I held my hand up, stopping him. "What exactly are you wanting to happen here?"

Ian slid his hands beneath the edge of my shirt, his fingers tickling my skin. "Whatever you want."

Breathing coming in short gasps, I started to put two and two together. "That's why you weren't worried about sharing me with your brother."

"What?"

"Have you shared women before?" I asked, watching Aidan's face for any sign of deceit.

"Yes." That one word boomed out of Aidan's mouth, and instead of angering me, made my insides melt into a gooey puddle.

"Does that bother you?" Ian brushed his cheek against mine, his fingers dipping into the top of my pants.

Shaking my head vigorously, my mouth dropped open.

“Good.” Aidan stopped before me and then, without warning, ducked his head. His mouth pressed to mine in a hot, aggressive kiss that left me gasping and soaking wet. He pulled away from me, but I practically jumped as I wrapped my arms around his neck, pulling his mouth back down to mine.

Ian chuckled as my legs crossed behind Aidan’s waist, his hands cupping my butt to hold me up. Thankfully, I was able to pull my mouth away before Aidan tried to take us to Trina’s bed.

“My bed’s that way.” I jerked my head toward the other side of the room.

Aidan redirected us toward mine. The last thing I needed was Trina griping at me for doing exactly what she told me not to ... not that I was planning on doing anyone today.

Sitting on my bed, Aidan pulled me into his lap. A second set of hands came up from behind me, slipping beneath my shirt to cup my breasts. When I didn’t protest, my bra was unsnapped, and bare hands held my sensitive skin. Pulling away from Aidan’s mouth with a gasp, Ian took the opportunity to pull my shirt over my head along with my bra.

A rumbling growl came from Aidan, his eyes locking onto my chest. Ian didn’t give him the chance to adore me for very long before he pulled me around to kiss me. His kiss didn’t last long before he was pushing me toward

Aidan. Confused but aroused, I let them maneuver me into Aidan's lap, my head tilted to one side.

Aidan's mouth immediately found the sensitive spot between my neck and shoulder, his mouth attacking it as his hands found my breasts. Half distracted by Aidan, I barely registered Ian unbuttoning my pants. When he started to pull them down my hips, I jerked up.

"Wait, hold on."

Ian stopped and glanced up at me for direction.

Torn between wanting to continue and fear of what could happen, I struggled to find my words.

"We'll go as far as you want. Just tell me if you want to stop." Ian met my gaze, the seriousness there stilling the anxiety inside of me. I leaned back and nodded, letting him resume his actions. He tossed my pants to the ground and reached toward my panties, and I was suddenly happy to remember that I'd worn cute ones and not my lazy grandma panties.

"Maybe you should lock the door first," I panted, his fingers inching closer to where I wanted them.

Aidan lifted my head up from my neck long enough to say, "Can't."

Shifting my hips to try and grind down on Ian's hand, I gasped, "What do you mean you can't?"

Ian paused his hand, causing me to growl in frustration. "Only the owner of the room can lock it."

At my curious look, Ian continued, even if, unfortunately, his hand didn't. "It keeps people from taking advantage."

"Gotcha." I thought for a moment and stared longingly at the bedroom doorknob. I could wish for the knob to lock but that seemed like a waste of a wish. Also, I couldn't find my shirt or bra right now, let alone that necklace. I also didn't want to move from the tantalizing position I was in. It might give the guys ideas of stopping.

Unable to forget about the chance of being interrupted again, I pushed out of their grasp and walked over to the door in only my panties. The whole way there I could feel their eyes on me. I locked the door with a flip of my wrist. When I turned back around the hungry expressions on their faces made me sway my hips just a bit more than usual.

Coming up to the edge of the bed, Aidan grabbed hold of my waist before I could decide where exactly I was before and sat me down in his lap. Something large and stiff rubbed against my butt, and I couldn't help but wiggle against it.

Aidan grunted, his grip tightening on my waist and urging me to lean back against him once more. My head lulled to one side, allowing

Aidan to find the spot on my neck that drove me crazy. My legs fell to either side of his massive thighs, leaving me open and dripping for Ian's attention.

Ian watched me in Aidan's arms for a moment, his eyes trailing over my bare breasts, my nipples pebbling at his gaze. Aidan's large calloused hands cupped my breasts as if putting them on display for Ian. The thought turned me one more than the actual act itself.

When Ian's hands came up to the edges of my panties, a startled sound escaped me. "Shh, now. You have neighbors. You wouldn't want to alert them," Ian murmured, pulling at the side of my underwear as I lifted my hips.

Gasping, my skin completely bare to the room, I asked, "Can't you do one of those silencer spell thingies?"

Shaking his head, so his hair brushed against my stomach making my muscles clench, Ian said, "No, another rule. Only you can." Ian dropped his mouth to my stomach, leaving hot open mouth kisses along my pubic bone.

My eyes rolled back, and my hands clenched Aidan's head behind me the further down Ian dipped. Getting a hold of myself barely, I breathed, "But I don't know that spell."

This time Aidan spoke. "Then you must be very, very quiet." He turned my face toward him, capturing my mouth with his just as Ian's mouth found my aching center, swallowing my cry. I tried to clamp my legs closed, but Aidan's thighs kept me from moving, leaving me utterly at their mercy.

Ian hummed against my core, his fingers dipping into me. Overcome by all the sensations, my hips bucked up against him on sheer instinct, urging him deeper inside of me. I let go of Aidan's mouth to catch my breath and bit down on my lip to keep the groan caught in my throat from coming out.

The closer I came to my release, the brighter the light in my mind's eye burned. Eventually, it felt like my skin was going to buzz off of my bones and I couldn't catch a breath. Right when I thought I was going to lose it, that it was becoming all too much for me, Aidan was there.

His hands laced with mine, his deep voice humming in my ear as he coaxed me toward my release. For some reason the chaos inside of me calmed at the touch and the sound of his voice, keeping it from burning any brighter.

Ian's mouth and hand moved quicker now, and that urgency to find my release came back with a vengeance. This time, nothing Aidan said could stop the light inside, and my hands tightened in his until I was sure I was hurting him, but he didn't utter a single word of complaint. Things low inside me tightened deliciously until I couldn't hold back a loud moan that came along with a flickering of lights.

I released Aidan's hands and sagged against him, my whole body feeling a bit like a loose noodle.

Ian sat up, wiping his mouth off with the back of his hand. "Now, that wasn't so bad was it?"

Still reeling from my high, I sighed and giggled. "I think you better teach me that spell."

Chapter 14

"I CAN'T BELIEVE YOU have not only one date for Valentine's but two and I don't even have one," Callie whined in my ear.

I grinned and adjusted the phone between my ear and shoulder. "You can't tell me that you don't have a line of guys just waiting to take you out for Valentine's." I grunted, digging through my closet for the matching shoes to the red dress I'd picked up last weekend with Trina. Paul and Ian were supposed to be here any minute to pick me up for our date.

"Not like you though," Callie pouted. "It's hard to want ordinary when you've already met extraordinary. None of these guys have magic wands or fingers."

I huffed a laugh and grinned. If only she knew what other parts of my guys were magical. Just thinking of what Ian did to me with his mouth gave me shivers.

"What was that?"

"What was what?" I asked, shifting the phone from one ear to the other so I could put on my shoes.

"That noise. It sounded like someone got laid and didn't tell me."

I rolled my eyes. "You can tell all that from a noise?"

"No, I just know you that well." Callie quieted for a moment and then when I didn't say anything asked, "So, which one was it?"

"Which one was what?" I sighed and stood.

I moved over to the mirror on the back of the closet door and smoothed my hands down my dress. The straps were made of lace and about two inches thick, coming down into a square neckline. It showed off just enough of my cleavage without giving away the whole show. The top stopped right under my bust and connected to the bottom skirt with a thin layer of lace, giving a peek-a-boo glimpse of my skin beneath. The skirt itself landed about mid-thigh while the lace overlay continued until just before my knee. I'd left my hair down and curled the ends, so they fell over my shoulders. I felt grown up and ready to go on my first adult date.

Usually, I would go with pretty over sexy, but call me optimistic. I wanted to look good for the Broomsteins. My initial hesitation about letting loose with my magic had been thoroughly squelched by Ian and Aidan's assistance, and I was ready to find out how far I could go before losing all control.

“Which of the guys did you let stir your cauldron?” I could hear the smile in her voice, and it made me grin in return.

“Sorry to disappoint but no one has stirred my cauldron.” I paused for a moment and then decided to give her a bone. “It did get a thorough cleaning though.” I grimaced at the metaphor, hating what I have been reduced to.

“I knew it!” Callie hooted, and I pulled the phone away from my ear with a pained wince. “How was it? And who was it? I bet it was Dale, it was Dale, wasn’t it? He seems like the type. He does run his mouth a lot, so I’d imagine he has quite a bit of practice with that tongue of his.”

I was so happy that Trina had already left for her date with Libby ... who she had finally asked out. I already had one best friend digging into me. I so didn’t need it from both sides.

“It wasn’t Dale.”

“Then Aidan?” She prodded and then hummed. “I could see that. He has that quiet strong protector vibe about him. Definitely a giver.”

I grinned, remembering how Aidan had touched me. Each brush of his hands was meant to give me pleasure and not a bad kisser either. Ian had been right about fighting my attraction to him. I and my body were extremely happy to have gotten over it.

"No, Aidan didn't, but he was there."

There was a pause on the other side of the phone and for a moment I had to look at it to make sure she hadn't hung up. Nope, still there.

"Callie?"

"Hold on, I'm envisioning it."

I rolled my eyes. "Whatever you are envisioning, please stop. It's creepy."

"What?" Callie scoffed. "I don't have four sexy wizards all hot for my body. I have to live vicariously through you."

"Well, maybe you should stop thinking about what you can't have and what you could have there." I moved over to my desk and pulled out my lip gloss, a red tinted shade to go with my dress. Moving over to the mirror, I reapplied it and then rubbed my lips together. "Are you still coming for Spring Break?"

"Of course! I wouldn't miss it for the world."

"Not even to go to the beach with your friends from there?"

"Pfft. What friends? You're my only friend. No one here gets me the way you do."

I faked a coo. "That's so sweet, but I'm still not telling you."

"Why?" Callie whined. I could practically hear her stomping her feet like a petulant child. "I thought we told each other everything?

You told me when you lost your virginity to Jaron."

"That's because he dumped me the next day." I frowned, not liking to talk about my first and only serious boyfriend.

"And I was there to pick up the pieces and remind you that he is a jerk wad who wouldn't know a good thing if he had it in his lap – which he did! Come on, I think I deserve something. I held your hand and spoon fed you Rocky Road ice cream for Christ's sake!"

Laughing uncontrollably, I shook my head and sighed. "Fine. Alright, you can stop guilt tripping me. It was Aidan and Ian."

The squeal that came from the phone made me jerk away from it. I could hear Callie's high-pitched voice crying out and talking at a rapid pace even with the phone a foot away from me.

Thankfully, I knock on the door – a rapid one, two, three – saved me from having to answer. I put the phone close to my mouth without putting it completely to my ear. "Sorry, gotta go." My response earned me an irritated rush of complaints before I hung up.

I grabbed my small black clutch, the only appropriate date night purse I had, and put my phone and my lip gloss in it. There was another knock on the door, this time a bit more urgent.

Turning the knob, I pulled the door open while trying to get my bag zipped up. "Sorry, Callie wouldn't stop talking my ear off."

"That's okay."

My head jerked up, my eyes widening with surprise. Instead of Ian and Paul waiting with me on the other side, Dale stood there looking way too yummy for a drop by. Clearing my throat, I shook off my arousal.

"Hey Dale, what are you doing here?"

Dale gaped at me for a moment, his eyes scanning me from top to bottom. I flushed under the attention he was giving me, happy I'd chosen the dress. "Wow, you look ... wow."

"Thanks." I ducked my head and leaned a hand against the door frame.

Dale cleared his throat and shifted from foot to foot. I noticed he had one hand behind his back and looked very much like a child caught with his hand in the cookie jar.

"I know we didn't make plans for Valentine's but ..." He moved his arm out from behind him, holding a single red rose in front of him. My eyes widened, and a soft smile curved up my lips. "I thought maybe we could get a bite to eat?"

My shoulders sagged. Crap. I didn't tell Dale about my date with the brothers. Now I had to figure out how to tell him I couldn't without hurting his feelings.

Not taking the rose from him, I reached out and touched Dale's arm. "As much as I would love to, I already have plans."

"Oh?" Dale's brows rose, and then they shot up even higher when he seemed to realize what I was saying. "Oh, I see you. I'm sorry I shouldn't have just assumed." His hand with the rose dropped to his side. "I guess I'll just talk to you tomorrow?"

He started to go, but I grabbed his shoulder before he could. "Look, I'm new to this and don't really know the whole precedent for the whole holidays and date thing when dating more than one person. I didn't think it would be an issue since you never brought it up."

"I know," Dale nodded reluctantly. "It's my own fault for not thinking to ask you earlier. I meant to, I did." Dale sighed and pushed his glasses further up his face. "My class work this semester has gotten my head. I'm so full of algorithms I barely have enough of my brain straight to brush my teeth. Not that it's an excuse to forget about you or Valentine's day."

"But you didn't forget." I gestured to the rose. "You're here. I should have told you I had planned a date. Can we do something later?" I held my breath, more anxious about Dale's reaction than I was about getting turned down.

Dale pressed his lips together tightly and nodded. "Yeah, sure. Sounds good." He moved to leave but then stopped and handed me the rose once more. "Oh yeah, this is for you."

With gentle fingers, I took the rose from him, letting our fingers brush each other. Before he could try and take off again, probably to go brood, I grabbed his wrist and jerked him toward me. He knocked into me, almost making me lose my balance in my heels. Automatically, his hands wrapped around my waist to keep me from falling.

Not giving him a chance to speak, I cupped his face and kissed him. He didn't react right away, his body stiff against mine. Then slowly, he adjusted our kiss, angling my head to the side as his hand tangled in my hair. I let go of his face and linked my arms around his neck, pulling him closer to me.

My skin warmed and I moaned into his mouth as one of his hands slid down to my butt. He pressed me to his front, the thin fabric of my dress making it even easier to feel the evidence of his arousal. My back touched the frame of the door as Dale's leg slipped between my thighs, lifting my skirt up slightly. A pulsating need started where his thigh rubbed against my center, and I rocked in response. A low whining moan released as Dale changed the pace of our kissing to that of his leg. I moved up and down against that leg, his tongue darting in and out of my mouth faster and faster. The ball of light in my mind's eye fluttered with excitement, but I didn't push Dale away this time. I hugged him closer to me, releasing his mouth with a gasp as my orgasm hit.

"Wow," I gaped at Dale who grinned. I was happy to see the hurt in his eyes had disappeared and, in its place, a smug male satisfaction.

"Well," a throat cleared, and a dark chuckle followed. "I'm feeling a bit shorted only getting dinner."

It was then I remembered where exactly we were and what we were doing. My face burned with embarrassment as I disentangled myself from Dale to face Ian and Paul.

Ian wore a pair of grey slacks and a matching suit jacket. A salmon-colored shirt was paired with a tie in a deep wine color. He paired his clothes with a sexy smirk and a hot leer as he scanned my rumpled form.

Paul had gone for a more classic look. Black pants, black jacket, white button-down shirt and a blood red tie. They were both deliciously wrapped and all mine.

Dale didn't shy away from me even when the guys stared on. If anything, he moved even closer. For a second, I worried we'd have a pissing contest, and I was the fire hydrant. Not exactly the way I'd imagined being sandwiched between the three of them.

I dipped my head and fixed my lip gloss that had no doubt smeared. Paul didn't say anything, his hands in his pockets as he watched us. A kind of silent jealousy permeated from him that I couldn't quite figure out.

"Did we interrupt something?" The bite to Paul's voice made me frown. He knew I was dating Dale as well, so the rudeness was uncalled for.

"Yes, actually," I shot him a warning look before holding the rose up. "Give me a second while I put this up."

Ian only watched with bemusement, probably not at all threatened by my and Dale's display. After all, he had seen me and tasted me. Paul, I could understand the frustration after a moment's thought. He seemed to get cockblocked at every turn. Seeing me with Dale probably felt like another shot to the gut.

However, I refused to apologize for them catching us making out in the hallway. Instead, I took the rose from Dale and sat it on my desk before coming back out of the room, closing it behind me. I kissed Dale on the cheek, earning me a heated look from him. "I'll see you later, alright?"

Dale cupped my face and kissed me once more, the intensity of it shot through my body and straight out of my toes. When he released me, I was breathless and more than a little aroused.

"Have a good night," Dale said to me, while to Ian and Paul, he warned, "Take good care of her."

"Of course, we will," Paul quipped, his tone not losing any of its edge.

"Thanks for warming her up for us," Ian shot back at Dale with a wink, his arms wrapping around my waist, ushering me down the hallway.

"No problem." I glanced behind me to get a final glimpse of him, and I was relieved to see the grin on his face and not a scowl like I knew Ian had hoped to cause.

The guys had given the impression that they were all okay with the way our relationship was set up, but I still worried if ... or when ... the other shoe would drop. I just hoped I had a full handle on my powers when it all went down.

Chapter 15

IAN AND PAUL LED me out of the school, each of my arms looped through theirs. Several people watched and whispered as we passed by, but I was grinning too broadly to care.

Let them look.

When they led me to the gate of the campus, I searched for a car, but there was nothing there save for a black carriage drawn by two pure white horses. Something was different about them though. I couldn't put my finger on it. Just different.

"Do you see it?" Ian whispered, dipping his head down to mine. He pointed at the horses, and now as if they knew we were talking about them their coats sparkled like diamonds. They shook their heads, and I swore something protruded from their heads.

"No," I gasped, taking a step toward the horses. Or should I say unicorns? "They're not real." I gaped and turned back to the grinning brothers. "Tell me I'm hallucinating."

“If you are then we are,” Paul chuckled and then glad bowed to the carriage door that opened on its own. “After you.”

Still in awe of the beautiful creatures pulling the carriage, I took the hand Ian offered me and stepped up into the carriage. I sat down on the plush red seat, my fingers sinking into the cushion. Little balls of light hovered along the top of the carriage, filling it with a soft glow. The girl inside of me sighed amorously.

Ian and Paul climbed in after me. There wasn’t enough room for them both to sit by me, but they seemed to have planned it beforehand. Ian sat next to me while Paul sat across from us.

It was when the carriage began to move that I realized there was no driver.

My hand shot out to the sides, one on the carriage wall and the other landing on Ian's lap. “Who’s driving this thing?”

Ian grasped my hand in his, and Paul chuckled as he said, “The unicorns, of course.”

My heart racing in my chest, I forced myself to relax. If they weren't worried, I shouldn’t be.

“How do they know where to go?”

“We told them.” Ian played with my fingers, stroking the tips of his along my palm, making a shiver run through me.

My lips ticked up at his answer. “And they just know?”

"Why is it so hard for you to believe?" Paul asked, crossing one leg over the other as he leaned back against the seat. "You easily accepted you were a witch and everything else, but the fact that a unicorn knows directions astounds you?"

"Give her a break, Paul." Ian brushed his hand across my cheek, giving his brother a warning look. "She can't help that her wildest little girl dream has come true."

I stuck my tongue out at Ian, shoving him playfully. "I did not dream about unicorns."

"Oh?"

"I dreamed of my own personal boy band."

Ian and Paul stared at me for a moment before bursting into fits of laughter.

"What? It's not that funny," I grumped, crossing my arms over my chest. "All the other girls were doing it."

"But I bet none of them grew up to be dating enough guys to form their own boy band." Paul bumped my foot with his, grinning from ear to ear.

I beamed and opened my mouth to ask a question.

Ian pointed at me with a lazy hand. "No."

I scoffed. "What? You didn't know what I was going to ask."

Shaking his head as the carriage came to a stop, Ian's eyes twinkled. "Yes, I do, and let me tell you now, neither of us has any musical talent. So, get any daydreams of us bringing your little girl dream to life out of that pretty head of yours."

I huffed and pretended to be offended. "I'd never do that."

"Sure," Ian drawled, moving to the carriage door that had just opened. He reached a hand toward me, leading me out of the carriage and onto a rose-colored carpet.

I stared up at the building, more like a palace really with its three stories and tall towers. Gorgeous bushes with roses of every color lined the white walls and long vines decorated stain glass windows. Soft music filled the air and the faint scent of baked bread wafted by.

"We're eating here?" I gaped at the castle before us. "I thought we were going to a restaurant?"

Paul stepped out of the carriage, offering his arm to me. "We are. We figured you'd probably had your fill of human restaurants. It's time to show you what our world has to offer."

Slipping my arm into Paul and Ian's, I asked, "What's it called?"

"The Palace," Paul said matter-of-factly.

I held back a laugh. "Of course, it is."

As we approached the double doors, they opened on their own, allowing the sounds of the restaurant inside to fill my ears. A maître d' waited behind a wooden stand much like a human restaurant except the mustache on his face kept changing its length at will. First, it was long like a wizened old wizard, then short and thin curling up at the sides. When he saw us approach, his mustache stopped on thin and flat against his lip.

"Mr. Broomstein," he nodded to each of the brothers. "We have been expecting you. Come this way." He gestured a white-gloved hand toward an archway leading into the dining area.

Dining area was an understatement. Ballroom was more like it, with a ceiling so high you'd need a fire truck ladder to clean the chandelier. Tables laid spread out through the room with a long stage like area filling one side and stretching into the middle of the room. Many of the tables were already filled, and the moment I walked in with the brothers, all eyes turned to us.

The maître d' paid no attention to me or questioned why I was with both brothers. He was probably paid to keep the secrets of the wealthy because this was definitely a rich person's place. I bet they didn't even have prices on their menus. Suddenly my nerves were going through the roof.

"Relax," Ian murmured into my ear, caressing the top of my hand.

Paul ducked his head as well. “Don't worry, this is all for you. We want you to enjoy yourself.”

Nodding dumbly, I allowed them to lead me to a table right at the end of the stage. My chair pulled out for me on its own, but Ian and Paul waited for me to sit before they sat down as well. I jostled when the chair pushed me up to the table, a menu popping into my hands out of nowhere.

Well, that was one way to do it.

When the maître ‘d left, a buxom redhead approached the table. She eyed the guys like they were something that was offered on the menu and hardly noticed me at all. “Hello, how are we doing this evening, gentlemen?” Her eyes slid over to me and she added as an afterthought, “Ma'am?”

Oh no, she didn't.

I know I didn’t look anywhere old enough to be called ma'am. The guys didn't even look up from their menus, completely oblivious to her drooling and veiled insult.

Having just about enough of her crap, I leaned toward Paul who sat on my right as I trailed my fingers up his arm. He turned his head toward me, and I brushed my lips against his before really capturing his lips with mine. I made sure to give him a really good, toe-curling, just short of marking him like an animal kiss, before releasing him. Clearing my throat, I dabbed at the corners of my lips.

"Hey now!" Ian wrapped his hands around my arm and pulled me toward him. "I'm feeling left out."

Batting my eyes, a coy grin curling up my lips, I cooed, "We can't have that, now can we?"

The way Ian took my mouth couldn't be called anything less than possessive. His fingers curled into my hair and angled my head to the side so that his tongue could ravage my mouth. When he finally released me, I was hungry and not for anything on the menu.

Ian shifted so that he was back in his own seat, picking up his menu like nothing happened. I lifted my own menu, glancing at it then up at the waitress. "I think we're gonna need a minute."

The waitress stared at me half like she wanted to pull my hair out and half like she wanted to be me. Shifting in place, she cleared her throat and dipped her head. "Certainly."

When the waitress left, Ian rolled his head toward me. "Do you feel better now?"

My face heated, and I ducked my head. "Yes."

"Well, we sure put on quite a show," Paul drawled, his eyes scanning the tables around us. "I'm not sure the performers tonight will be able to beat us for the Witch's Weekly headline."

I twisted in my seat to see the couples who had come for a quiet romantic Valentine's dinner had started to take pictures and text rapidly on their phones. Yeah, we had put on a show alright. A front-page runner.

The waitress came back after a few minutes to take our orders, but this time she was all business. Short and to the point, she was borderline rude before she marched away haughtily.

"So, what's this show you were talking about?" I asked just as the lights began to dim.

Ian took my hand with a grin. "Just watch. You haven't seen real magic until you've come to The Palace."

A spotlight shone in the middle of the stage where a small man stood in a suit. A piano began to play as the man began to speak. His voice projected throughout the room though he had no microphone that I could see. "Ladies and Gentlemen, thank you for choosing to spend your Valentine's Day at The Palace. We have a lovely performance for you tonight. Just for our lovers."

Paul took my other hand at the man's words, each of the brothers watching my face as I watched the stage. What was going to happen that they were so excited for me to see? I shifted in my seat and waited with growing excitement.

“Please, sit back and relax. While The Palace and its dining room presents ...” the brothers and the rest of the dining room sans me laughed, “... your dinner.”

As a cheerful song began to play, several other people came out onto the stage with the announcer. They began to dance around the stage, dressed in chef’s hats and carrying trays full of food. As they sashayed and paraded around, singing their song, I began to get a bit bored. This was what they were all so hyped up about?

All of a sudden, the dishes on the table joined in the fun, causing me to jump in my seat, my hand going to my chest. The dishes, even the salt and pepper shakers, spun around and did a sassy jig. I leaned in toward the ketchup bottle and poked at it. The bottle jumped back like I’d hurt it, and I swore that if it had hands, it’d have hit me. It sure looked like it wanted to tell me where to stick it.

“Chill out, it’s just a spell,” Paul assured me, and I settled back in my seat for the rest of the show. The performance just kept surprising me. Champagne bottles popped their corks, spewing forth their bubbly insides in large arches over our heads. I flinched but realized none of it was going to fall on us.

When the music ended, our food appeared just like magic. Sometimes it’s good to be a witch.

Chapter 16

AN INCESSANT RINGING WOULDN'T let me go back to sleep. I had been dreaming about ice cream, cherries, and very naked wizards covered in whipped cream. I'd been just about to find a banana when the ringing started.

"Hello?" I grumbled my eyes still closed as I answered the phone.

"What are you still doing in bed at this hour?" my grandmother's voice admonished me, and even though it was through the phone, I could just see her disapproving frown in my head. "It's already past ten o'clock. Any proper witch would be up by now."

"Well, I guess I'm not a proper witch," I sassed into the phone, rubbing my eyes as I sat up. "Did you want something?"

Grandmother huffed and, thank all that was good and decent, let my sleeping habits go. "I was calling to see if you had taken any consideration into letting us sponsor your booth for the fair? It's only a few weeks away, and it does take quite a bit of preparation to have everything arranged on time."

Scratching my head, I tried to process her words. I hadn't really thought much about my booth, not since before Paul had given me a lesson on the magical government. I had kind of found myself at a standstill. I knew what I wanted to use as my main theme for my booth, but not really how to go about it. Also, the sponsor part had me stuck.

"I have thought about it, and I don't think you are the right person to help me with this." I could practically hear her head exploding on the other side even as her voice came out calm and put together.

"I understand your hesitation. You don't know me, and I haven't given you a very good impression of us so far, but I want to make it up to. Please, allow me to help."

The genuine tone of her words caused a wave of guilt to rush through me. I hadn't really given her much of a chance, not that anyone could blame me with the way she had reacted over several issues. However, if I was going to be in the magical community, I had to figure out some kind of middle ground. What better way than to join together for a cause?

"If I say yes, what do you want in return?" My experience told me I shouldn't expect her just to help for no reason.

"Why, nothing of course. You're my granddaughter, I want nothing more than to help you succeed."

"I see."

"But since you were offering," which I wasn't, "you could see our sponsorship as a sort of payment for letting me provide you with a coming out party this summer."

And there it was.

I slipped out of my bed, my eyes going to Trina's bed. It was empty. Not surprising, she usually went for a run early in the morning. Another one of her traits I just didn't get, but as long as she didn't try to make me go with her, we didn't have a problem.

"And that's it? I let you throw me a coming out party, and you'll sponsor my booth?" I couldn't help the suspicion creeping into my voice.

"Yes, that's all."

I sighed in utter defeat. I just hoped my mom never hears about this.

"Fine. It's a deal."

"Excellent," my grandmother exclaimed on the other line, drawing my attention back to the conversation at hand. "Now, you said you were going to major in political science, have you figured out your platform?"

"Yes," I smiled, anticipating her reaction when I told her. "I want to discuss the need for a better transition method for human-raised witches and wizards. Those like me."

There was silence on the other line for a moment, and I thought I might have caused her to have a heart attack.

"Grandmother? Are you there?"

"Yes, yes, I'm here. My apologies." She cleared her throat, and I could just see her trying to control her face and not tell me how she really felt about human-raised children. "I think that is a wonderful idea, my dear."

"You do?"

"Yes, we have needed new regulations for quite a while now, what better way to push those who refuse to change than this?" There was quiet again for a moment before a fluttering of paper could be heard on the other line. "You will need some kind of slogan, something that will really catch the eye of the community. And of course, we'll need to create merchandise, buttons, t-shirts, mugs, the works. I hope I can count on you to create the booth and gather all the information you need to present your argument for this?"

I gaped at the phone, surprised she had gotten on board so easily. Gathering my wits, I quickly nodded my head. "Yes, I've got that part down, though I might need a bit help on the exact language to use."

"Not a problem. Just let us know how much you need for the booth and any other questions you might have. Maybe we could get together for dinner sometime? Go over all of the details?"

"Okay, that sounds good."

"Wonderful. I'll have my assistant look at my and your grandfather's schedule and get back to you. Have a good day."

"Uh, yeah. You too." My brows furrowed as I hung up the phone. Well, that had been an odd conversation.

Now fully awake, I had no choice but to get up. I had planned on sleeping the majority of my Spring Break away, at least until Callie got here. She wouldn't let me hide away like the hobbit I longed to be. She would be here sometime today, and would no doubt start her interrogation process, nagging me until I gave her every detail of what has happened between the guys and me. I wondered what she'd think of my date with the brothers.

The date on Valentine's Day with Paul and Ian had been an eye-opener into the magical community. It really showed me what it could be like with us out in public. While it had its downs – nosy witches and wizards – it did have its perks.

Thankfully since then, Paul and Ian had buried whatever hatchet they had going on and even had plans to throw a party together tonight. Of course, I was invited, and that meant I'd have to bring Callie along. Maybe I could find her some wizard hottie to distract her from my love life. God knew she needed another hobby besides me.

Gathering my toiletries and clothes, I headed to the co-ed shower down the hall. The school was mostly deserted with most of the students had gone home for the week-long holiday. Trina and I had both decided to stay back. For me, it was because my parents weren't even home. Dad had to fly to California for some speech and mom had tagged along. Trina had told me she'd rather not have to share a bathroom with her siblings if she could help it, not that I blamed her. The co-ed shower was bigger, and even though you had to share them with other students, it had to be easier than having your little brother or sister barging in on you all the time.

When I entered the bathroom, I was happy to find it empty. I got the whole place to myself which meant I got to pick whatever shower I wanted. That included the much-coveted shower on the end.

Unlike the other showers, this one had a wall as a barrier for two sides while the rest of them had curtains. It was a far cry more private than the one-sided showers, plus it had the best water pressure. No one wanted to wash their hair with barely a spritz.

Stripping quickly, I jumped into the shower, turning the heat up to volcanic levels. Sighing as the water poured over me, I found myself humming a popular song I'd heard on the radio. I wasn't that great of a singer, I'd never have my own record deal or anything, but the soap bunnies have never complained about my singing.

Halfway through my shower, the curtain pulled back, and a waft of cold air hit me. I clutched my washrag to my girly bits while my arm shot up to cover my breasts. When my eyes hit Dale's amused grin, I scowled.

"Warn a girl, geez! I could have broken my neck." I threw the rag at him, hitting him right in the face.

Shutting the curtain behind him, Dale chuckled. "But what a lovely corpse you'd be." His eyes trailed down my naked form, and it was then that I realized he was lacking in clothing as well. My eyes dipped down over his lean but chiseled chest and lingered on the red puff of hair surrounding his hard length.

Licking my lips, I gulped. The carpet did match the drapes.

"Did you have any doubt?" Dale guffawed, coming closer to me until I had to lift my gaze.

"Did I say that out loud?"

"Yes, you did." Dale reached out, and I prepared myself to be ravished, but he grabbed my shampoo I had hanging in the basket on the wall.

A bit put off at him being in the shower with me all naked and wet but not even interested in doing anything naughty, I tried to snatch it back from him. "Hey, now that's mine."

"But I didn't bring mine."

"So not my problem." I wrinkled my nose at him as I strained to get it. "Maybe you should have thought of that before invading my quiet time." I nudged him with my elbow and turned away from him, pretending like he wasn't there. Not like that was possible. Even not looking at him, I could feel the heat coming off of him and then, as he stepped just an inch closer, the tip of him brushed against my butt.

"I heard a dying kitten and had to come to investigate. I had no idea that thing being tortured was you singing."

Face screwed up in annoyance, I whipped around to give him a piece of my mind but ended up backed up against the shower wall. A shiver raced through me as the cold tile wall touched my back while my front turned to molten lava from the press of Dale's body against mine.

"I thought we might finish what we started on Valentine's Day?" Dale's words caressed my lips, but not going the final inch to kiss me. "We never did get together afterward, not how I wanted anyway." His hand on my waist dipped down between us as he rubbed the washcloth I had thrown at him against my center in a long, languid movement. My mouth fell open, and my head bumped against the tiles behind me.

"What do you think?" Dale asked, his fingers pressing against me through the washcloth.

What did I think? I thought I wanted that washcloth off and his hands really on me. That's what I thought.

I didn't say that, however. Instead, I took the initiative and found the hard, pulsating flesh bumping against my thigh. This time, Dale let out a long-strangled moan as my hand moved up and down him in a rhythmic motion. The washcloth dropped, and Dale's hands braced on either side of me, his hips jerking into my grasp.

The door to the showers opened loudly, and voices echoed in the bathroom. I paused my hand movement for a moment, listening to the group of females that had come in.

"So, I heard the Broomsteins are having a party tonight. Are you going?" one of the females asked.

Dale's hooded gaze met mine and I grinned coyly, starting my hand up again. The females continued talking, not knowing what was currently going on in the last stall.

"Of course, Paul is so hot," a different one said this time. My hand stuttered.

"No way. Ian is the sexy one. He had that dark and broody bad boy thing going for him." There was a giggle and a slap of hands.

One of them snorted. "Good luck getting anywhere with either of them. They're so wrapped around that Mancaster girl's fingers."

"Yeah, what a slut."

"You know, I heard ..."

My hand had all but stopped moving at this point, and Dale let me know not by making it move but by dropping one of his down between my thighs.

I gasped and then stifled it quickly. My eyes locked on his as I moved my hand once more. Each tug earned me a delicious circular movement from Dale, and soon, I wasn't paying any attention to what the females were saying. It took all I had to control my breathing and not make any kind of noise while Dale and I drove each other to our peaks.

The showers next to us turned on just as I came, a small squeak coming out of me. Dale's hand quickly covered my mouth, but it was too late.

"Hello? Are you okay in there?" the first female asked in the stall next to me.

Removing Dale's hand, I lowered my voice a pitch and said, "I'm fine. Water got cold."

"Ugh, man that sucks. I always use the temperature control charm to keep my water at just the right heat."

"Thanks, I'll do that next time." I turned off the water and grabbed my towel, pushing Dale away so that I could look outside the stall. No one was out there, so I wrapped myself in my towel, grabbed my things, and hurried out of the bathroom like hell itself was chasing me.

I barely made it to my room before I ran into someone. A group of students came around the corner just as I shoved my way into my bedroom. Slamming the door behind me, I sagged against it.

Trina sat on her bed with her tongue down Libby's throat, just adding to my embarrassment. Pulling away from her, Trina took in my half-drowned rat look and lifted a brow. "Bad shower?"

I shook my head and breathed deeply. "Don't want to talk about it."

"Well," Trina stood up, pulling Libby up with her. "I'll let you get dressed. Meet me downstairs for lunch?"

"Sure, sounds good." I set my things on my bed and watched as they left. Libby only gave me a cursory glance before leaving, and I had only just dropped the towel on the ground when the bedroom door opened again, revealing Dale. His hair was still wet, but he had put his clothes back on. He must have used a spell of some kind because he wasn't wet anywhere else on his body and trust me, I was looking very closely.

His eyes swept my form, and a devilish grin curled up his face. Pulling his glasses off his face, he came toward me. "Now, where were we?"

Squealing as he came toward me, my scream turned into a giggle as he tackled me to the bed. Our mouths came back together in a rush of tongues and hands. I dragged Dale's shirt over his head as he pulled loose my towel. Releasing his mouth reluctantly, I gasped my eyes, rolling back in my head from the hand cupping my breast.

"You're perfect," Dale growled into my skin his mouth trailing down my neck. "How is that possible?" He cupped both of my breasts, bringing them together in the middle and laying a kiss on each one of them.

I chuckled at his actions. "Believe me, I'm far from perfect."

"Watch your tongue," Dale quipped as he gave me a warning look. "I've never seen a more exquisite pair of breasts."

"And you've seen many?"

Dale's face flushed, and he stuttered over his words. "No, I mean, I didn't mean to imply I've been with a lot of women. I just—"

I giggled and brushed his hair away from his face. "Calm down, I was just messing with you. Now, you, on the other hand ..." I trailed my fingers down his chest to the band of his pants. "... have plenty to be proud of." I jerked on his belt and unbuttoned his pants. I had just got my hand down his pants when there was a knock on the door. I didn't have a chance to tell them to hold on before the door burst open.

"I'm here, I'm fabulous, and I'm ready to find myself a magical hottie," Callie sang as she barged into the room. Her eyes widened so much I thought they would pop out of her skull as she took in the scene.

"Callie," I growled as she continued to stare. "Callie!"

"Right, sorry." She slapped her hand over her eyes and turned her back. "You know you should really lock the door."

I looked up at Dale, giving him an apologetic smile. Eventually, we'll get all the way there, but it wasn't going to be today.

Chapter 17

"CALLIE, JUST DROP IT," I groaned and resisted the urge to bang my head against the side window of her car.

"I can't," Callie whined, smacking her hands against the steering wheel. "I've been begging to get all the nitty gritty details of your sex life, and here I am, cockblocking you like a big fat jerk."

"I don't have a penis, so I don't think you could do that even if you wanted to," I pointed out, making her nose scrunch up.

"Clam jammed?"

"No. And the point is that nothing was going to happen. So, you don't have any reason to feel bad."

"Your hand was down his pants, and you were naked." Callie raised a brow at me and then added, "Bushwhacked?"

"Oh my god," I moaned, rolling my neck. "If you promise to stop doing that, I'll introduce you to some hot wizards at the party, okay?"

"Deal. Hold on tight." Callie beamed at me and sped up.

My hand automatically gripped the side of the car, my eyes squeezing together tightly. After Callie had barged in on Dale and me, the mood had pretty much been killed. So, Dale told me he'd see me at the party and left me to Callie. Now, I was wishing I'd gone with him to the party rather than letting my best friend drive. I'd be lucky to get there alive now.

"So, have you done it with any of them yet?" Callie asked, pulling up to a gated palace with an intercom system. Her question was left unanswered as both of our mouths dropped open in awe.

I'd never been to a palace, but if anyone asked me what I thought one looked like, the Broomstein estate would be it. At three stories high, it had large paned windows and red brick covering the entire outside. The driveway looped around in a u-shape and was already packed full. Every light in the house seemed to be on, but if anyone came to investigate, they'd think no one was home. There wasn't a single sound coming from the house, not even a car engine revving.

They had left the gates open, so there was no need for us to get buzzed in, but the moment our car pulled through the gates and into the driveway, a weird sort of pop filled my ears similar to the silencing spell Paul had done before. Where the house had been quiet before, now it was booming with life. Music poured out of the open front door, and the crowd filing in full of excitement for the party inside.

"Woah, what was that?" Callie asked, putting a finger in her ear and wiggling it around.

I smiled until my cheeks hurt. "Welcome to the magical community. If you think a silencing spell is impressive, you haven't seen anything yet."

Callie returned my grin as we climbed out of the car and headed toward the door. Ian had told me it was a pool party, so it wasn't unusual to see the other guest entering in only bathing suits and wraps. I had a feeling he picked the theme so that he could get me naked again, but I wasn't about to make it easy for him.

I opted for a pair of short jean shorts and a tank top over my yellow bikini. Callie didn't share my opinion and wore a sheer pink cover over a purple bikini, gold chain-link pieces holding the top and bottoms together.

When I asked her why she would want to wear something that would burn her in the sun, she'd said, "Beauty is pain, love. Beauty. Is. Pain."

Bunch of boloney.

We moved into the house arm in arm, our eyes widening even more at the inside of the place. The large chandelier took up most of the entryway ceiling, each piece sparkled in the light, and my eyes strained the longer I stared at it. Besides the chandelier, the next eye-drawing piece was the expansive staircase. I could just see a Cinderella type coming down those stairs. Everyone would stop and stare at the gorgeous mystery woman, then a handsome prince would wait at the bottom of the stairs anxious to ask her to dance.

And my prince – well, one of them – was leaning against the end of the staircase. Besides the fact that this was his house, Ian looked the like he was in his element. Wearing his usual black t-shirt, he eschewed the jeans for black swim shorts. His hair looked like someone had been running their fingers through it, and the long lashes that surrounded his hazel eyes were slightly glazed. He'd clearly already started drinking.

When Ian's eyes moved from the guy he was talking to and found me, a slow, sexy grin curled up his lips. He said something else to the guy and moved toward me. The crowd didn't so much as part but shifted with his movements, like a snake slithering through the grass. When Ian came within reach, his arms wrapped around my waist, one hand settling on the swell of my hip.

“Hello, beautiful.” He leaned down and pecked me on the lips. I could smell the liquor on his breath and feel the sway of his body against mine.

“You are quite drunk.” I chuckled and tapped a finger on his chest.

“Drunk on you,” he sang, twirling me around in a circle. I met Callie’s eyes with their raised eyebrows as I spun.

Laughing, I stopped Ian from pulling me into a more involved dance and grabbed Callie’s arm. “Hey, Ian. This is Callie, my best friend. Callie. Ian.”

“Callie!” Ian grinned at Callie and wrapped his arms around her, hugging her before spinning her in a circle. When he put her back down, they were both laughing, and I couldn’t be happier.

“Nice to meet you.” Callie moved back to my side, her eyes scanning him up in down in a cursory way, not a sexual one. “At least you have clothes on.”

Ian quirked a brow at me.

I made a face at him but didn’t explain. Instead, I bumped Callie’s shoulder. “Callie here is in need of a hottie of the magical variety. You got any suggestions?”

His brow furrowed in such an adorable way, I ached to be alone with him and see how else the alcohol affected him. However, I had to be careful not to voice my wishes since I’d taken the initiative to wear my wishing amulet. If anything, it would help me get Callie something and then she'd stop hounding me for details.

"I think I have someone she might like." He turned over his shoulder and shouted, "Hey, Griffin." A brown-haired guy with a strong jaw line and large biceps came barreling down the stairs.

"What's up?" His voice had a growl to it that I could tell effected Callie physically. At his appearance, she had immediately shifted her stance, cocking one hip out to the side, her other hand twirling in the hair hanging over her shoulder.

"This is Callie." Ian pointed a finger at Callie, causing the guy to turn his attention to her. His eyes moved up and down her form, heat filled his gaze, and he licked his lips like a wild lion ready for dinner. "Callie, this is Griffin. Griffin's majoring in magical criminology and can bench press a car."

"Now, that's a lie." Griffin shoved Ian on the shoulder but took a step closer to Callie. "But I can bench a lot." He picked up Callie's hand and pressed his lips to the back of it.

Callie giggled and batted her eyelashes. "I bet you couldn't bench me."

"Oh, I'll take that bet." He dragged her away and into the crowd. Callie giggled and glanced back at me, giving me a thumbs up sign.

“Think she’ll be okay?” I asked Ian, letting him pull me into a slow dance.

“Oh, she’ll be fine. The same kind of spell at the dorms was put all over this house. He can’t do anything against her will.” He traced his fingertips down my shoulder, along my arm, and laced them with mine. We moved from side to side along with the music, and everyone else faded away.

“What about you? Bring many girls here? Is that what the spell is for?” I asked in rapid succession, staring up at him. I watched his lips move as he went to form his words. Usually, he was quick to answer, but with the drinking, it was taking him longer to form his thoughts.

“No, but we have quite a few parties here, it only makes sense. Keeps everyone involved safe.” One side of his lips curled up, and his eyes dipped down to my tank top. “Now, you are dressed completely wrong for this party. How are you going to swim in this?” He fingered the strap of my top.

I smacked his hand and grinned. “I have a suit underneath. You just want an excuse to see me take my clothes off.”

“Can you blame me?” Ian leaned down and brushed his lips along my neck and then nipped my earlobe. “You’re addicting. I’d love to get another taste of you.”

My body warmed at his words. I hummed and bit my lower lip. "Well, maybe we'll have to find some time to give you another dose."

When we were just about to kiss, a hand pulled us apart. "Do you mind if I cut in?" Paul came between us, looking just as delicious but much soberer than Ian.

"Sure," Ian chuckled and patted him on the shoulder. "If I can't share with my brother, who can I share with?"

I giggled, but Paul's lips barely twitched. Hmm. What's his problem?

"I'm going to make the rounds. You take care of our girl." Ian gave Paul a knowing look before disappearing into the crowd.

Paul didn't take Ian's place in the dance, instead standing there with his hands in his jean pockets. He was one of the few who wasn't dressed for the party. The tense setting of his shoulders told me something was on his mind.

"So ...?" I shifted in place, trying to start the conversation. Maybe find out what was eating him.

"You look really good." Paul gestured to my outfit and then rubbed the back of his neck.

"Thanks."

"I saw Callie found someone to sink her hooks in already." Paul nodded his head in the direction Callie had gone.

"Yeah, now maybe she'll be less interested in who I'm sleeping with and more interested in her own love life." I laughed and then rolled my eyes. "Not likely but one can dream." Paul's lips curled upward into a smile. "There it is. Finally."

Then the frown returned.

"What?"

I crossed my arms over my chest and stared him down. "Are you going to tell me what has your panties in a twist, or are we just going to keep making awkward small talk?"

Paul smacked his lips and looked around the room. "Not here. Too many ears."

"Alright." I gestured with my hands for him to lead the way.

He took my hand and pushed through the crowd, leading us up the large staircase. When we hit the top of the stairs, a weird rubber band-like feeling came over me. The sound of the party muffled but didn't completely disappear, not like it did at the gate.

"What was that?"

"A barrier spell. It's just to keep the party downstairs and away from our bedrooms. It helps to keep random people from finding a bedroom not their own." He shot me a grin and a wink, the first one I'd seen all night.

We went down a hallway and turned left, before finally stopping before a door. Opening the door, he waved me inside. The room smelled like him, mahogany and vanilla. It even looked the way I thought it would look, with deep rich colors and a wall full of books. The four-poster bed took up the majority of the room, the duvet a sapphire blue.

"I love your room." I twisted around to face him, only to find him inches away. Licking my lips, I swallowed. "Hey."

"Hi," Paul took my waist and drew me to him. I placed my hands on his arms, waiting to see what he would do. Surely, he didn't bring me up here just so we could … you know.

His lips brushed against mine in slow sweeps, but as much as I wanted to let him deepen the kiss and see where the night would go, something was bugging him, and that took precedence.

"Paul," I pulled my head away and shifted out of his embrace. "We're supposed to be talking."

Paul let out a frustrated growl, dragging a hand through his hair. "That's the problem. We always just talk. I've talked to you more than I've even kissed you and I got there first. That's the crazy thing. You kissed me first." He paced back and forth in front of me as he ranted passionately.

"Hold up a second." I held my hands up, waving them to get his attention. "So, the reason you're all bent out of shape is that we haven't done anything more than talk and kiss a bit?"

"Right."

I sighed and dropped my hands. “Paul, you’re not jealous of the other guys, are you?”

“No,” he shouted and then lowered his voice. “No. I’m not jealous of you seeing them. I’m more ... disappointed by the outcome of our encounters.”

“What? You lost me.”

Paul scratched the back of his head and grimaced. “It seems like I’m always getting you hot and ready only to have you fall into another man’s arms.” I tried to speak, but he stopped me with a hand. “Now, I don’t blame you. I know my school work along with my TA job has made me fairly busy. And I take fault in that. However, it doesn’t dismiss the fact that—”

“You’ve gotten the short end of the straw.” I finished for him with a small smile. “I get it. I do. I’m having a difficult time juggling my own class work and four guys.”

“Four?”

I winced. “Ah, yeah. Aidan has now been moved up from cute stalker to sexy man meat with great hands.” I grinned at the memory of what those said hands had done to me.

“Right,” Paul drew out with a nod. “So, another one to get further than me.”

“Well,” I shifted toward him with a coy flutter of my lashes, “we’re alone now. There’s a barrier on the upstairs so the only people who could interrupt us would be ...?” I played with the neck of his t-shirt, pulling my bottom lip into my mouth with a grin.

"Ian or a member of the household."

I fingered my necklace brushing my collarbone. "I have something that could help with that part."

Paul's gaze dipped to my necklace. "The wishing amulet? What would you say?"

I thought about it for a second. What could I wish to give Paul and me a chance to get closer? Well, what was the problem really? Every time we started getting somewhere, we got interrupted, or Paul had to go to work.

So, what we needed were time and privacy. Now, to word it so that it didn't bite me in the ass. No need for another Sabrina incident. I couldn't just ask the amulet to get people to leave us alone because that could end up with us being alone for five minutes or forever.

Tricky, tricky.

"I wish no one would come looking for us or enter this room for …" I raised my brows at him. "… an hour?" I stated it as a question, but the necklace warmed immediately. I clucked my tongue. "Well, I guess that worked. We have an hour. Think that's long enough?"

Paul grinned, pulling me to him. "I'll make it work."

Chapter 18

THERE WAS ONE THING I could say about the Broomstein brothers. They were givers all the way. However, they each had a different style to it.

Where Ian liked to tease me until I exploded, Paul was all about getting as many orgasms out of me in a short period of time. It might have been the short time frame I had wished upon us, but I couldn't complain.

"No more," I gasped, tugging on his hair to drag him out from between my legs. "I surrender."

"Are you sure?"

I laughed at his apprehensive expression. "If I had a white flag, I'd wave it."

Paul crawled back up my body so that his lower half laid between my thighs. His hard length brushed against my sensitive skin, and I let out a moan, caught between pain and pleasure. I now believed death by orgasm was a thing. A great, wonderful thing.

Kissing me lightly, Paul reached between us and shifted his hips. I came out of my delirium long enough to put my hand on his arm. "Hold on. Do you have any condoms?"

Paul's brow furrowed. "No. I don't use condoms."

I gaped at him, pushing him away in horror. "What do you mean, you don't use condoms? Everyone uses condoms."

Shaking his head, Paul moved to sit on the edge of the bed. "There's a potion girls take for that. I never had to worry about it with ..."

Jealousy flared in me. "Sabrina, you mean? You never had to worry about using a condom with Sabrina." Now I really was worried. So much for the mood, it was thoroughly smashed. With a disgusted growl, I climbed out of the bed and began pulling my clothes back on.

"What are you doing?"

Shoving my hair out of my face, I glared at him. "What does it look like? I'm done here. What a waste of a wish," I muttered, jerking my shoes on with angry force.

Paul rushed around and cut me off before I could hit the door. "Come on, don't leave. Just because I don't have a condom like a stupid ..."

"Keep talking, Paul." I snapped, snarling in his face. "Just keep going. You're doing a great job of making sure you never see me naked again." I spun around and reached for the doorknob.

"Look, I'm sorry." Paul grabbed my arm. "I've never dated someone who was raised as a human. I didn't know I'd need to prepare something, or I would have."

"And you just assumed I'd be on something?" I quirked a brow, crossing my arms over my chest. "Despite what the rumors are spouting about me, I've slept with a total of one person. One." I held up my finger and shoved it in his face. "Forgive me for not jumping onto birth control the morning after when he dumped me!"

Paul's face had a mixture of horror and pity. That was the final straw. Jerking my arm away from him, I marched out of the room and hurried down the hallway before he could stop me again.

I didn't run into anyone on my way back through the maze of a house. Luckily, we hadn't turned too many times for me to find my way back to the staircase and the raging party below. That rubber band feeling came over me as I popped out of the private area, and the music blared loudly in my ears.

Rushing down the stairs, I searched for Callie or even Trina, who I had yet to see at the party. When I didn't see them amidst the dancing guests, I headed outside. The music was just as loud out here, except the lights were dimmed to allow for a kind of sexy ambiance.

The massive pool was filled to such a capacity that I feared someone might drown from all the writhing bodies. The water changed colors on demand as bubbles were created out of nothing, floating up and into the night sky. If I didn't know any better, I'd say that it was a regular old college party, except for the bathing suits covered in dancing pineapples and the random swirls of multicolored sparkles floating in the air without any kind of wire attached to them.

I now understood the need for the bubble around the property. If a human came wandering in to investigate the noise, there'd be all kinds of hell to pay.

I passed by a couple of people making out on some lounge chairs, searching around for Callie's familiar blonde head of hair. A squeal pulled my attention to the pool once more.

Callie's blonde head came sputtering up from beneath the water, a playful irritation on her face as she splashed the perpetrator. Griffin laughed and wrapped his arms around her waist, dragging her to him. They backed up against the side of the pool and proceeded to make out.

Well, there went my ride. I so was not getting in the middle of that. I'd never hear the end of it.

Turning away from the pool, I bumped into someone's cup, and it all came spilling out onto my jean shorts.

"Sorry," the girl whose drink I spilled on me grimaced.

I shook my head and proceeded to pull the wet shorts off. "It's my fault. Don't worry about it."

"You know, I know a spell that would dry that right up."

The familiar sound of Dale's voice had me spinning in place. I launched myself into his arms and buried my face in his neck. Inhaling him deeply, I could feel the stress of the night melting away.

"Hey!" Dale patted me on the back, holding me tight. "I'm glad to see you too."

Tears pricked my eyes as I held onto him. I didn't want to move away. I didn't care who was watching, I just wanted him to hold me for a moment.

"Max." Dale eased me back, wrapping an arm around my shoulders as he led me to a chair in a more secluded part of the pool area. After sitting me down, he brushed my hair away from my face, his thumb smoothing across my cheek where a tear had escaped. "What's wrong? Did something happen?"

I shook my head, turning my face away from him. "It's not important."

"Well, it sure seems that way. You're crying." Dale thankfully didn't try to turn me back to face him. I hated crying. I wasn't a pretty crier, and I didn't want him to see me this way. He smoothed his hand along my hair, his voice low and soothing. "You can tell me. I've been told I'm a good listener." He huffed a laugh, making me smile slightly.

Sniffing, I twisted around, my eyes down at my hands. "I think I just overreacted." I sighed heavily. "Am I wrong to get jealous over an ex when I'm the one forcing four guys to date only me?"

Dale's thumb pressed my chin up, urging me to look at him. "No one is forcing anyone to do anything. I promise you, we all want to be here. We want to be with you."

"But why?" I grasped his hand with mine. "What's so special about me? I'm nobody." Dale started to interrupt, but I beat him to it. "Okay, so I have famous grandparents that don't mean anything to me, and if anyone wants to be with me solely for that reason, they might as well hit the road."

"So, money and fame aren't things you value?"

"No."

"Did you know that Aidan, Ian, and I were best friends in elementary school?" Dale said out of the blue.

"You were?" my eyes widened. "What happened? I mean, between you and them?" I left out the obvious reasons that Ian and Aidan were still best friends. I mean, they pretty much tag teamed me in my room.

Dale lifted a shoulder. "What usually happens. We drifted apart, became interested in different things. Also, their parents weren't that happy about them hanging out with someone like me."

"You mean someone without any magical status?"

"Yeah. So, it might not mean much to you, but most of the people here ..." He gestured around the party, where no one was paying much attention to us. They were too busy focusing on their own entertainment. "... they care. Being with you not only makes them look good to their peers but could open doors for them in the magical community they might not have had otherwise."

"So, you think that Ian, Paul, and Aidan only want me for that reason?" Anger and hurt swelled in my throat, my eyes burning once more.

"No."

My head jerked up to meet Aidan's hard gaze. His form loomed over Dale and me, covering us in shadows.

I forced down my anger long enough to ask him, "No? What do you mean no?"

Aidan knelt before me, drawing the attention of those around us. He didn't seem to care though. "I did not know your name before I saw you in my mind. I only saw a beautiful woman with a laugh that lit up the sky." He took my hands in his large ones. "I knew once I met you that I had to know you." Aidan's lips caressed the top of my knuckles. "Nothing and no one would have kept me away."

Wow. That was what I called romance. Who knew a man of so few words would have that kind of passion inside of him? The fact that he had been watching me before we even met, maybe even before I came to school, should have freaked me out but it didn't. It made me feel confident that someone wanted me for me and not for my grandparents' name or money. He made me feel wanted.

My mouth dry, I wetted my lips before opening my mouth to speak. "So, your stalker tendencies weren't because of my winning personality?"

His lips curved at the edges. "No. They were not."

Dale cleared his throat, interrupting our moment. "You know, you can't really keep calling him a stalker when you also call him your boyfriend. It will confuse people."

I glanced from Dale to Aidan. "He's right. You have touched my boobs, after all." I grinned and giggled, earning a heated look from Aidan.

"Come on, the party's just started." Dale stood and offered me a hand. "How about a drink?"

I stared at his hand and then to Aidan. Aidan stood as well, also offering me his hand. With a huff and a smile, I placed my hands in both of theirs and let them pull me to my feet. Those who had been watching before had already turned their attention back to their own conversations. No one even cared about us anymore. We were yesterday's news.

Aidan and Dale ushered me over to the bar they had set up outside by the pool. I didn't really drink, but I allowed Dale to order me something and push it into my hand. I took a small sip of it and made a face.

"Not good?" Dale asked with a laugh as Aidan watched me with bemused eyes.

I scrunched up my nose and shook my head. "It's bitter and kind of burns."

"Is this your first time drinking?" Dale took the cup from my hand and gave it back to the guy working the bar. I lifted a shoulder in response. "Okay, how about this, instead?" He then asked the bartender, "One Bubble Pop."

"What's a bubble pop?" I wrinkled my nose as he passed me the drink. The liquid was pink, it fizzled, and it smelled like a strawberry lollipop. I took a tentative sip. It also tasted like a strawberry lollipop, and the burn was barely noticeable.

"Good?" Dale asked, watching intently.

I nodded, taking another big drink of the tasty concoction. Each drink made my body warm and tingly as it settled in my stomach. I giggled and then hiccupped. A pale pink bubble came floating out of my mouth, hovering in the air. When I leaned in closer to look at it, it suddenly popped.

"Oh! So, that's why it's called Bubble Pop." I giggled a bit again on the incessant side. Was I drunk? Already? I'd barely had a drink. I couldn't possibly be drunk that fast.

"Come on, lightweight." Dale wrapped an arm around my waist and led me inside, Aidan close behind.

"Hey, Max!" Trina cried out, waving her hand high in the air, as she came barreling toward me in a lime green bathing suit. The sides were cut out with a thin strip connecting the middle, showing off a swirling tattoo along her side.

For some reason, I lifted my hands up in the air too, shouting, "Trina!" When I got close enough, I wrapped my arms around her, pulling her into a tight hug and jumping up and down.

"Okay, okay," Trina laughed nervously, pushing me away. I hung onto her shoulders as she asked Dale, “How much has she had to drink?”

“One,” Aidan said simply.

“Not even one.” Dale corrected.

Trina took the cup Dale had in his hand and sniffed it. “Bubble Pop! Come on, you don’t give a Bubble Pop to a lightweight and a human raised one at that! You have to start out small.”

I wiggled my finger at her face, my body swaying from side to side. “Bubbles are fun.” I hiccupped again, a bubble floating out of my mouth. “Look, look!”

“Yeah, that’s great,” Trina said, not nearly as excited as I was. Why wasn’t she happy about the pretty bubbles? In fact, she looked downright irritated.

“We’re taking her to get some water.” Dale dragged me out of Trina’s arms, and I flopped onto him, grabbing his glasses from his face.

I put the glasses on and cocked my head to the side. “Look at me, I’m Dale. I have a stick up my bum but have mad kissing skills.” I giggle-snorted as Dale took his glasses back and then handed me over to Aidan. “Oh, I need a big strong man to save me. Are you that man?” I squeezed his biceps with a saucy waggle of my eyebrows.

Aidan chuckled, the sound rumbled through his body and shook mine. Bending down, he slipped his arm under my knees and then the world was upside down.

"Let's go, princess."

My head bounced around, and the world danced as we moved through the crowd. I felt like I was flying ... until I saw a blonde that even upside down and, even drunk, I recognized here. Lifting my head quickly, something I regretted immediately, I watched Sabrina come down the stairs from the private section with a smug expression on her face. Paul came hurrying after her, tucking his shirt into his pants.

"Put me down." I smacked Aidan's arm when he didn't listen. "I mean it, put me down now!"

Aidan brought me back down to my feet, a confused expression on his face. I stared hard at Paul and then Sabrina and then back to Paul. His gaze met mine, confusion and hurt filling them before he looked to Sabrina and back to me. At that, his eyes widened, and his mouth dropped open.

I turned away from him just as he yelled my name. Grabbing Dale's arm, I pulled him toward the entrance. "Take me home. Now."

Chapter 19

I REALLY WANTED TO wish it all away. However, I only had three wishes left. I needed to start being more careful about using them. My last one was a complete waste of time and magic.

Taking a deep breath, I held it for a moment and then let it out with a long sigh. Bringing my arms down to my sides, I shifted on my yoga mat in the middle of my and Trina's room.

I'd spent most of my time in the room since the party. I knew it was childish, but I couldn't face Paul, not after what happened at his house. Worse, if I left the room, I could run into Sabrina. That was the last thing I needed. She'd waste no time rubbing in my face how she got Paul right after I'd run out on him.

Sucking in another breath, I lifted my hands over my head and stared up at the ceiling. Then again, maybe it was my fault. I lashed out at him like an immature brat rather than discussing it like a rational adult, but no, I had to be the jealous crazy woman because I didn't know they didn't use condoms.

You know what? I blamed my mom. It wasn't my fault. She didn't tell me. She should have prepared me.

And how would that have gone?

Oh, hi, mom. I want to have sex with all my boyfriends. Are there any differences I should be aware of? Like maybe contraceptives?

"Let the air out already," Trina snapped from her desk, slamming her pen to the table. "You're starting to look like Smurfette."

Letting the air out in one fell swoop, I dropped my arms and glared at her. "I do not. I didn't even get light headed."

"Well, it freaks me out. You need to find some other way to de-stress. You've been doing way too much yoga, and it's frankly annoying. No one needs to be that limber." She gave me a lopsided grin and a wink.

Shaking my head, I bent down and rolled my mat up. I shoved it under my bed and then pulled the tie out of my hair, letting it fall to my shoulders. The release of my hair made my scalp feel all tingly. Maybe I had been doing too much yoga.

I flipped open my Potions book to where I had been reading. I was just about done with my paper for the final project in Potions 2. I just had the paper's conclusion to work on, and it would be good. Unfortunately, thousands of words and I still wasn't anywhere near confident in my ability to create the dang thing.

Guardian Light, my ass. I could use a Guardian Light just to make it.

"Are you going to the lab later?" Trina asked.

I glanced over my shoulder at her. "Uh, yeah. Probably. I don't know. Might just wait until later tonight."

"You really think the cover of darkness will lower your chances of running into Sabrina or Paul?"

"What? No. Of course not." I faked surprised, but the way my voice went up an octave clearly gave me away. "Okay, fine. I admit. I don't really want to run into either of them. Sabrina for obvious reasons. Paul … I don't want to listen to whatever excuse he has, and I know he has one."

"Well, you didn't exactly let him explain," Trina said with a pointed look.

I shot her a look. "Whose side are you on?"

"Yours, of course, but still, it's hardly fair. You see something, you're not even a hundred percent sure of what's going on, and then you go running out. Now, you refuse to talk to him. You should give him a chance to explain."

"Why?"

"Because, do you really want to leave things this way especially since you are boning his brother? Might make holidays awkward." She picked her pen back up and gave me a knowing look before turning back to her desk.

Frowning, I hated to say that she was right. If I was going to date Ian, then I couldn't very well let things fester with Paul. However, right now, I needed one more book from the library before I could head to the potion's lab to attempt my possibly life-changing project.

Gathering up the books I already had, I shoved them into my bag and headed for the door. With Spring Break pretty much over, the hallways were filled with students settling back in for school to start. I half-hoped I wouldn't run into anyone I knew on the way to the library, but I didn't count on it.

I patted my bag where I'd tucked my wishing amulet away. I was tempted to use one of my wishes to make sure I didn't have to talk to Sabrina or Paul. No, I made it get this awkward, I had to face it like a grown up.

And here was my chance. I stifled a groan as Sabrina sauntered my way with Monica and Libby in tow. I braced myself for impact but was completely baffled when she didn't do more than shoot me a look like she smelled something bad. She'd probably tell me that it was me if I asked.

"Hey, Monica." I nodded at the brunette who stopped to talk to me.

"Max, I haven't seen you around lately." She fiddled with her gold hoop earrings with a smile. "I saw you at the Broomsteins, but you disappeared before I had a chance to say hi."

I grimaced. "Uh, yeah. Bubble Pop incident."

Monica hissed. "I completely understand. Those things taste so good, but what you don't realize is that the magical properties of it make it equal to having three shots of vodka in just one sip."

"Holy crap." I gaped and shook my head. "I'm going to kill Dale."

Laughing lightly, Monica shifted in place. "Well, I've got to get going. We're going to grab a bite to eat before we settle in for a big study night. You're welcome to join us."

My eyes slid from Monica to where Sabrina and Libby waited. Libby seemed completely oblivious to everything around her. Sabrina caught me looking and used her middle finger to scratch her nose.

I gave a weak smile, almost a wince. "Uh, that's okay. I'm going to attempt my Potion assignment."

"Ah, yeah. I heard you got Guardian Light. That blows. Would be cool if you make it work though."

"Right?" I laughed. "Anyway, I'll see ya."

We waved and parted ways.

Before I could hit the library, my phone rang. Pulling it out, I glanced down at the screen and groaned. Grandmother. Great.

"Hello?"

"Maxine, I hadn't heard from you about a time to meet, so I thought I would take the initiative and call you." The *again* was unspoken but clearly implied.

I tugged my bag further up onto my shoulder. "Uh, yeah. Sorry about that. I've been so busy with school and ..."

"Partying at the Broomstein estate?"

I clamped my mouth shut. How the heck did grandmother know that?

"People talk, even in the magical community." She sniffed. "Especially in ours. If anything, it moves faster. Plus, the Broomsteins are our closest friends, and the sons always throw a party around Spring Break."

"Oh." I relaxed. "Yeah, I went to that. Not that great."

"I see. In any case, if you could send me the list of items you need for your booth, I will be sure you get a check from us for the amount needed."

"I will."

"Have you worked on your speech?"

"Yes, I have it taken care of."

I didn't need to ask her which one she was talking about. The contest required me to write a paper explaining why I should receive the award as well make a small five-minute speech explaining my platform. Not too much work for a whole year of college paid for.

"Good. You are far more prompt than your mother ever was when it came to her school work. It was like pulling teeth trying to get her to finish a project. Always hopping from one thing to another." She let out a long breath. "Well, in any case, I am proud of you for taking the initiative to help out your situation. The offer still stands, by the way, if you change your mind."

I cleared my throat. "No, I'm alright. Thank you."

"Very well. We still need to get together to discuss your coming out party. Perhaps you could find some time in between your school work and extracurricular activities to come by the house for dinner? You could even bring that friend of yours. Callie."

I resisted the urge to laugh at the disdainful way she said Callie's name. It was clear Callie's heritage kept her from getting my grandmother's approval, not that Callie would care, but I had to give grandmother some credit for even mentioning a normal human's name in relation to me.

"Sure, I'll find some time and let you know."

"Good. I'll see you at the fair then."

I said my goodbyes and hung up the phone. Tucking it in my back pocket, I made my way to the library. Talking to my grandmother made me realize I was being childish. If I wanted to get ahead, I had to make sacrifices which might mean doing things I didn't want to do. Like the coming out party. It also meant I couldn't hide any longer. I had a potion to make and a book needed to make said potion. I only hoped I could avoid Paul and Sabrina for a little bit longer.

There weren't a lot of people littered throughout the large room. Most were probably still recovering from their Spring Break fever ... or more like hangovers. It was great for me in any case. That meant the book I needed might actually be on the shelf.

I headed toward the potions section where I'd spent the majority of the last few days scouring for my project. I had all the books about the Guardian Light potion, its history, *The Ten Biggest Mistakes Made When Making a Guardian Light*, and now I needed the step-by-step process for creating the potion on a short time limit.

Most people who attempt the Guardian Light took several days to prepare and create the potion, which would then be spelled into the hovering ball of light. I did not have several days to prepare and create my little glowy guardian thing. The project was due next week, and with classes and the fair coming up, I didn't have much time to spare on the long version.

I tapped my finger along the spines of the books, making my way down the aisle. I reached the place I had seen the book last and came up empty-handed. My brow furrowed tightly.

"What the ..." I growled and stomped my foot. The book was right there two days ago. I couldn't do my project without that book.

In a frustrated huff, I fumbled with my backpack and pulled out my amulet. If this didn't count as an emergency, I didn't know what did. Rubbing the amulet, I muttered to myself, "I wish I had the book *Guardian Light Express* by Eli Guardian."

I didn't know what I was expecting, maybe some magical poof and the book appearing in my hands, but nothing happened. I just looked like an idiot standing in the middle of the aisle waiting for a miracle. Then what my dad told me came back to mind. The amulet couldn't create things out of nothing. So, my wishing to have the book wouldn't make it pop out of nowhere, especially if someone else had it. They would have to bring it back.

"Oh, uh, sorry." My head turned so fast that I feared I had whiplash from the movement. Paul stood at the end of the aisle with a cart full of books, an anxious expression on his face. I stared at him with my mouth hanging open like a guppy.

Snapping my mouth closed, I twisted the rest of my body around to face him. "Did you need to get in here?"

Paul played his fingers against the metal handle of the cart. “Yeah, but I can come back. It’s fine.”

“No, no.” I came toward him, chewing on my lower lip. “Go for it.”

I moved to the side so that he could push his cart by. As he moved in front of me, his scent filled my nose and my throat clogged with emotion.

Come on, Max. Get a hold of yourself.

“Thanks,” Paul said once he got by.

“No problem.” I shifted awkwardly. I watched him for a moment as he floated books onto the shelves. He didn’t say anything and barely even looked my way. Fuck it. Dropping my bag on the ground, I stomped over to him. “So, you’re just going to pretend like it didn’t happen?”

Paul glanced up from the book he was setting on the shelf. “I thought you didn’t want to talk about it? That is why you have been avoiding me right?”

I flushed. “I haven’t been...” Paul gave me a pointed look. “Okay, yeah. I’ve been avoiding you but what did you expect? We just almost ... you know ... and then you come out tucking your shirt in with Sabrina looking way too satisfied. What was I supposed to think?”

He pressed his lips together and then clucked his tongue. “I could see how you would think that, but if you had waited and let me explain instead of taking off, you would know that the only reason for Sabrina was up there was because she was asking me for help with her booth for the Spring Fair. That's it." He floated a book up from the cart and toward the bookshelf. I snatched the book out of the air and tucked it under my arm, forcing his attention back to me.

"But why did she even have permission?"

Paul sighed. "We did date you know. It was left over from then. We just haven't gotten around to removing her access."

Okay, so that made sense. I couldn't really fault him for that. And Sabrina was smug about many things. Me jumping to conclusions like that was just asking for trouble. No wonder she didn't mention it to me in the hallway.

"But why would she even enter the Spring Fair? She doesn't need the money." Panic and irritation filled me at the thought of having to compete against Sabrina. She'd had twelve years to think about her major and prepare for it. I haven't even had a year.

Paul shrugged. "She likes competition."

"And did you say yes?"

"I told her I'd see what I could do."

"Oh."

An awkward silence filled the aisle as I shifted before him. I wanted to discuss what happened in the bedroom but didn't know how to bring it up without making it seem like it was entirely my fault. Yes, I'd been a bit out of line freaking out the way I had, but he'd been wrong too!

"About the other night," Paul started, tucking his hands in his pockets and rocking on his heels. "I shouldn't have just assumed you'd be on the potion or pill or whatever."

"And I shouldn't have assumed you'd have a condom." I rushed to add in, ducking my head slightly.

"Still, when you have magic at your disposal, STDs and pregnancy aren't really that big of a deal. They figured out how to take care of those things a long time ago." His lips curled up on one side in such a cute but sexy way, making my heart beat sped up.

"Oh, cause we all know Merlin was such a playboy," I joked, laughing awkwardly.

"Yeah," Paul chuckled.

"Yeah," I repeated back, swaying from side to side. "Well, I'm glad we got that cleared up."

"Yeah, me too." Paul rubbed the back of his neck and grinned at me. "Do you think we could try again?"

My face heated, and a hot desire began to settle low between my thighs. I very much wanted to try again. "Sure, I'd like that." I then remembered why I was there in the first place. "If I can pass my Potions class anyway. You don't happen to have *Guardian Light Express* in there do you?” I glanced down at his cart, searching for the book I needed.

Paul chuckled, a sparkle in his eyes as he pointed at me. Confused, my eyes dipped down to the book in my hand. Laughing, I held the very book I needed up. “Well, look at that. Wishes do come true.”

Chapter 20

"YOU WANT TO SLOWLY add the fairy dust to the boiling liquid," Paul instructed me, standing over my shoulder in the potions lab. "Not too fast," he reminded me before I could even get the bottle over the cauldron.

Lowering my arm, I glared at him. "No one likes a backseat driver. Stop micromanaging me. I have to do this myself."

Paul gave me a sheepish grin, scratching the back of his head. "Sorry, I can't seem to help myself. Potions is my major after all."

"Yeah, I know," I said flatly. I turned back to the potion and slowly poured in the fairy dust, something I didn't know existed until recently.

The recipe for the Guardian Light potion included one cup of witch hazel – insert eye roll here - a pinch of sea salt, three white angel trumpets, plucked not minced, all mixed together and brought to a boil. Once boiled, it was time for the final ingredient, a bag of fairy dust. I was skeptical about the bag of fairy dust part. It didn't really sound like any kind of measurement to me, but apparently, they have little bags of dust about two inches tall that they get from the fairies, something that still blows my mind.

Not as much as this potion though. It had been so far so good up until this point with Paul hovering like a mother hen behind me.

If I poured the fairy dust in too fast, then the potion would foam and turn a sludge-like consistency. Too slow and it would boil over, turning a mustard yellow. Right now, it was a nice yellow-white, exactly how it should be.

Holding my breath, I poured the fairy dust one grain at a time into the potion. The liquid began to glimmer and sparkle, a sweet flowery smell coming from it. When I dumped out the last grain, I let out the breath I was holding.

"There," I wiped my forehead with the back of my hand and smiled up at Paul. "Now, just to let it simmer for two hours, then bottle it up and turn it in."

Paul lifted a brow. "You're not going to activate it?"

I shook my head, pulling my phone out to set a timer. "No, Professor Bromwick wants me to do it in front of her so she can be sure I did it right. Also, if it didn't, I probably will need a Potions Master to help me. I've read some weird accounts of potions gone wrong. I don't want to end up with an extra arm or something."

Chuckling, Paul wrapped his arms around my waist bringing me to his chest. "Good idea." Humming slightly, he pressed his forehead against mine. "So, two hours?"

"Right."

"What could we do during that time?" The hungry look in his eyes caused a warmth to spread down low. I barely had a chance to nod before his mouth was on mine.

Our tongues tangled together, and I slid my hands into his hair, tugging him close to me. Paul's hands moved down to my butt, cupping me against his hard front. I groaned into his mouth, feeling his need pressed against my stomach. Paul backed us up until my back hit the table opposite of my potion.

Lifting me up, Paul sat me on top of the table. My legs spread so open that he could step between them. Fingers played underneath the edge of my top, inching up as if afraid I would stop them. Pulling away from his mouth, I jerked my shirt over my head, dropping in on the ground next to us, followed by my bra.

Paul's gaze devoured my front, making me ache even more for him. Instead of touching me though, he moved away from me and toward the door. Frowning, I started to ask him where he was going, but he simply locked the door and turned on me with hooded eyes.

"Now, where were we?" he growled, his voice heavy with desire.

Before I could blink, he was back in front of me, his mouth trailing down my neck and then down to my breasts where he cupped them in his hands, bringing them up to his mouth. Either he grew more hands or was using magic because my pants unsnapped on their own. I lifted my hips, and this time, Paul released my breast and pulled my pants and panties down together, barring me to the lab.

Nervous but excited, I spread my legs for him but then snapped them shut again. Paul gave me a curious look, and I grinned. "Your turn. I want to see some skin."

Chuckling darkly, Paul pulled his shirt over his head, revealing his delicious muscles to my hungry gaze. Next came his pants and boxer briefs. His length bobbed before me as if he were saying hello.

Licking my lips, I reached for him, but Paul moved away from my touch. I frowned at him, but he only smirked.

"Patience, little witch." Reaching into his pants he had discarded on the ground, he pulled out a foil package. "I learn from my mistakes."

Giggling, I took the condom from him. "Actually, we don't need it."

"We don't?"

I shrugged a shoulder. "After our fight, I asked Trina about that potion. I figured that if I'm dating four guys, I probably should have gotten on it before. Thankfully, it isn't like human contraception and works right away."

Paul came at me like a starving lion, and I was the gazelle. He climbed onto the table, causing me to lay back on the top.

"Cold!" I cried out, pushing him back off me. "So cold."

Frowning, Paul stroked his jaw before snapping his fingers. The cold lab table beneath me lowered and stretched out to both sides until it was the size of a full-size bed. The hard-cold grey top sank beneath me, turning into a soft mattress.

"That's better." Paul nodded and then crawled onto the bed, urging me further up onto it. Recapturing my mouth with his, he made short work of getting me worked back into a frenzy. His fingers played me like a fiddle, and I was more than ready to take him as he plunged into me.

"Oh," I gasped, bucking my hips up to meet his thrusts. "Oh, god."

Paul grunted, his hand reaching between us to stroke me, causing my insides to clench tightly and my eyes to roll back into my head. I cried out as my orgasm caught me by surprise. Paul continued to thrust into me, and

I found myself building up to that edge once more.

This time when I came, the whole room shook as stars burst behind my eyes. Paul stiffened against me, a low groan coming from him as he reached his climax.

He didn't move right away but rested his forehead against mine as we caught our breath. "So, was it better or worse?"

"Huh?" I blinked up at him.

Leaning back onto his arms, Paul stared down at me. "You said you'd only done it once before. So ..."

I grinned, wrapping my arms around his shoulders. "Better. Definitely better."

Paul beamed with male satisfaction, and I felt him stiffen inside of me once more.

"Again?" I gaped and then moaned as he began to move. "I don't know if I can again."

"Don't worry, I've got you." Paul pressed his lips to mine, his movements quickening. He wasn't as gentle this time around, and I found myself hitting that peak way quicker than I expected, crying out for more.

I didn't know how many times we did it before we finally collapsed onto the table made bed, exhausted but satisfied. We laid together, basking in each other's bodies until a shrill beeping caused us both to jump up.

Realizing what it was, I moved off the bed to put my clothes on. "Potion's ready!"

Chapter 21

I TRIED TO MAKE the meeting with my grandmother at a neutral place, like a restaurant or café. Somewhere there were plenty of people, and my chances of escape were high. However, she insisted I come to their house and have dinner.

If I had thought the Broomsteins' house was big, this was nothing compared to that. The Palace was close but not quite. It had been just a tall building, most of it made for the actual restaurant. Mancaster Estate, on the other hand, was exactly that: an estate.

You couldn't see much of the house from outside the gates, but I could tell it filled a large portion of the grounds. I was sure there was more to it than just what I saw from the front. Maybe our family even had their own personal graveyard.

I didn't have a car of my own, but I didn't tell my grandmother. I knew she'd want to send a car for me and I couldn't have that. I was trying to make people like me for me, not my family name. Having a personal driver show up at the school would only contradict that effort.

The taxi I had hired pulled up to the wrought iron gates. There was no voice box to buzz me in. However, after sitting there for a moment, the gates opened on their own. The taxi pulled into the large u-shaped driveway, and I could feel the magic slip over me as we entered. It wasn't the same as the privacy barrier Paul had at his house or like the silencing spell. It was something completely different. I'd have to ask my grandparents about it.

Before I could exit the taxi, an older butler type came rushing out of the house, opening the door for me and offering me a hand out. I took it reluctantly and paid for the taxi. The driver bolted out of the driveway like hell itself was on his heels.

"My name is Oscar," the butler told me, leading me into the house.

"I'm Max," I told him, half distracted by the inside of the house. Inside the ceilings were high and open. It made the inside look even more humungous than they already did. A chandelier filled the entryway and stairs rose up on either side of the room to the next level.

"Yes, you are expected. Master and Mistress Mancaster are waiting for you in the sitting room," Oscar stated so matter-of-factly that some might have considered it rude. I just saw it as boredom. He obviously loved his job.

Oscar led me to the left into a large room with a fireplace and couches spread out tastefully. My grandfather sat in an armchair, reading from a newspaper that's words changed every few minutes. Grandmother wasn't in the room yet, but I was sure she'd come running when she found out I was here.

"Master Mancaster, your granddaughter has arrived," Oscar announced with a sort of bow. Wow, they weren't kidding about the royalty thing.

I inched around Oscar with an awkward look at his half-bowed form and took a seat on the couch across from my grandfather.

Taking his glasses off, grandfather waved Oscar off. "Max, it's so good to see you. I was afraid you might not come."

"Well, I couldn't say no," I gritted through my teeth. I understood now how my mom had such a hard time getting away from my grandmother. That woman could have been a lawyer in a past life.

Chuckling, my grandfather nodded. "Yes, your grandmother does have a way of getting what she wants. In any case, I am happy to have you here, no matter the circumstances."

I relaxed slightly. While my grandmother might be pricklier than a cactus at times, my grandfather knew exactly how to put someone at ease. “I’m happy to see you too.” I glanced around the sitting room. “Your house is so ... big.”

Laughing once more, he leaned forward folding the moving paper in his lap. “Well, at one time, we had enough people living here to need all this space. However, now it is just your grandmother and me.” His eyes twinkled as he added, “Perhaps one day you’ll live here and make use of the many empty rooms.”

I gave a noncommittal sound and then straightened as my grandmother came into the room. I never thought I would be happy to see her.

“Maxine,” she greeted with open arms. I stood and let her hug me, awkwardly patting me on the back. “It’s so good to see you. I hope you found the place alright?”

“Yes, the taxi driver knew exactly where it was.”

“Taxi!?” My grandmother placed her hand on her chest her eyes wide. “Why on earth did you take one of those wretched things?”

“Well, I don’t have a car ...”

My grandfather shifted in his seat toward me. “Max, we have a driver. They could have picked you up, no trouble at all.”

“I know but ...” I tried to think of an unoffensive excuse, but my grandmother cut in.

"Next time, we'll send a car for you ... or would you like your own vehicle?" She raised a brow and then turned to my grandfather. "Henry, maybe the blue one. The one that looks like a bug."

"I'm fine," I protested. "Really."

"Nonsense." Grandfather grinned, casting aside my response. "You're our granddaughter, it's only right we spoil you. Please take the car." He reached up in the air, and a pair of keys appeared out of nowhere. I stared at them as he held them out to me. "Here, no strings. I promise."

I glanced between them and my grandmother who watched with an expectant look. Geez. Put a girl on the spot. However, if I didn't take the car, it would set a precedent for the whole dinner. I was already swimming in tension, I wasn't sure I could handle any more.

"Fine." I sighed and took the keys from him. "Thank you."

"Well, now that's settled, dinner should be about ready. Let's adjourn to the dining room." Grandmother clasped her hands together before gesturing toward the doorway she had come through.

I stood and followed them into the dining room. Grandfather took a seat at the head of the table with grandmother at his right hand. Another place was set up on his left, so I sat there. I stared down at the long table and smiled to myself.

"What's that smile for?" my grandmother asked, catching me in the act.

My grin dropped, and I cast my eyes down on my plate. "Oh, nothing. Just ... your dining room reminds me of The Palace."

"Oh, you've been?" My grandfather picked up his water glass, sipping from it.

Before I could answer, my grandmother sniffed. "Of course, she has. She was on the front of Witch's Weekly the week of Valentine's."

I blushed. The guys had mentioned something about it, but I didn't think it was true. No one at school had said anything, so I figured they had been exaggerating. Apparently not.

"Ah, yes," my grandfather mused. "I remember now. You went out with the Broomstein brothers. Lovely young gentlemen."

I nodded. "Yeah, I like them a lot."

"And are you still seeing those other boys?" my grandmother asked, a hint of tension in her voice. At least she was trying.

I sighed. "Yes, I am."

Grandfather chuckled, startling me. "Good. It's good for a young girl your age to keep her options open. You're a Mancaster. Don't ever settle for less than you deserve."

I didn't bother correcting him on either account. It would just cause trouble, and I wanted to get out of here with my ears attached to my head.

"Well, I hope you are focusing on your studies as well." My grandmother unfolded her napkin and placed it on her lap, not meeting my gaze.

"Yes, of course." I nodded. "I actually just finished my Potions assignment for the semester. I had to make a Guardian Light."

"Really?" My grandfather shifted forward in his seat. "I heard those are rather difficult. I've never had to do one myself, but they can be quite useful."

"It was. However, I haven't activated it yet."

"Why ever not?"

"Professor Bromwick wants to evaluate it beforehand. We'll activate it on the last day of school." I smiled slightly. "Less likely to have some kind of accident."

"Sounds reasonable." My grandmother folded her hands in front of her. "Now, about the booth for the Spring Fair. What are you going to make it out of?"

Wiggling in my seat, I frowned. "I guess wood. I mean, that's what most are made out of, right?"

"Very well." A pen and paper appeared out of nowhere and started to jot down notes for my grandmother. “Are you planning on decorating this booth?”

“Well, yeah. My topic is pretty controversial, so I figured a nice calming color would help make people more accepting toward it. Come at it in a passive kind of way, rather than shoving it down their throats.”

Nodding her head, my grandmother started to speak but then stopped as a young redheaded woman came in and announced dinner was ready. The plate in front of me filled up with a roast that smelled so good that my stomach rumbled fiercely.

“Looks wonderful, Anita. Thank you,” my grandfather grinned at the young woman. “Well, let’s dig in as they say.”

I didn’t have to be told twice. The meat didn’t even need to be cut, it just fell off onto my fork. I popped it into my mouth and held back a moan. So good. The potatoes and carrots weren’t half bad either, each one filled with succulent juice and just soft enough.

“Besides, the wood – you can use a spell for the paint – how about pamphlets? Posters? Maybe even some kind of sign pointing at your booth?” My grandmother named things off in between bites.

“Pamphlets and poster are good, but not so much the sign. I mean, I’m going for subtle, not ‘look at me, look at me.’ Don’t you think the sign would contradict the feeling we're going for?"

"I agree," my grandfather said, taking a drink to swallow the food in his mouth. "The subtle approach is best for these kinds of things. Too many elitists are too stuck in their ways. The only way you are going to get them to listen to something like this is to slide it right under their nose with the promise of it being good for them."

"It is though," I insisted. "I mean, some might argue that we keep all human-raised kids out of our schools and eliminate the problem altogether, but then you have witches and wizards with no idea how to control their powers and causing all kinds of havoc. But, with my plan, we can catch them up and lessen the likelihood they would become a burden on society. No one wants to spend all day every day cleaning up uneducated kids' messes."

"Right." My grandfather shoveled another bite of roast into his mouth.

"Now, about your coming out." My grandmother said all of sudden as if she had been waiting for the moment to pounce. "I figured we could do it around your birthday. It's July 2nd, correct?"

"Yes."

"Then we can combine the two and make it a real affair. You'll need to make me a list of all your friends you want to invite."

"Okay."

"Also," she paused and locked her eyes with mine, "you need an escort. One. Not four. I leave that decision up to you."

Swallowing thickly, I jerked my head. "Okay. I can do that."

"Wonderful." My grandmother smiled smugly and continued to cut into her food. "I will take a look at my calendar, and we can set up a weekly meeting to go over things for the party. Please bring your mother if she is able."

I forced a smile. "I look forward to it."

Chapter 22

"WHY EXACTLY IS IT called the Spring Fair again? I'm melting out here," Trina whined, wiping her brow. She lifted the sides of her yellow tank top beneath her coverall shorts, trying to fan herself off.

"It's barely seventy degrees. Stop your griping." I bumped her with my shoulder. We'd been out in the courtyard since early this morning putting together my booth, and the sun had just gotten high enough to start beating down on us.

"I'm just trying to understand why we didn't make the booth inside and then bring it *outside.*" She pointed her hammer in my direction. "And don't give me that crap about it being too heavy. You have four boyfriends. Four. If magic can't help, then at least their combined muscles would get the job done.

"Yeah, I know, but I didn't feel right asking them to help me with this. Also, I don't want to risk something happening to it between the school and here." I gestured toward where Sabrina had already set up her booth, something about keeping magic for the elite, and was now lounging in the sun like she didn't have a care in the world.

With my potion's assignment done and turned in the only thing left I had to worry about was the Spring Fair. Well, that and keeping the peace between my parents and grandparents. Once I had my booth set up and the pamphlets I'd created talking about the benefits of creating a new system for human raised witches and wizards, I'd be ready to go.

Well, ready save for my speech. I had written it out on note cards and memorized it just in case. When the judges came around, I felt that I would be amply prepared for their questions. I just hoped it was enough to get me the winning vote.

"And we're done." Trina jumped up and holstered her hammer into her pocket like it was a gun. We stood back to get a good look at our work and frowned.

"Something's not right."

"Yeah," Trina tapped her chin with her finger. "Something is missing." Her eyes widened, and a smile covered her face. "I know." She closed her eyes for a moment and then clapped her hands together. The off-putting brown color of the booth melted away, and a soft blue took its place. "That's better."

"Much."

Sighing, I went to my box full of stuff for the fair and flipped through it. I had several posters to hang up behind us and on the walls to draw attention to the booth. I didn't just have to win over the judges but the people too. If no one came to my booth, I would lose points. I had to be able to persuade people not just with my words but with my presentation.

Sabrina had a flashy neon sign that pointed to her booth and could be seen across the courtyard. However, I was banking on the fact that she was focusing on the elite crowd and was completely snubbing everyone else.

Besides Sabrina and me, several other students were competing in the same contest. I didn't know most of them, and their topics ranged from saving the magical wildlife to getting more choices in the cafeteria. Sabrina really was my top competition.

"So, do you need me for much longer?" Trina asked after we finished putting up the posters. "I wanted to go find Libby. We're supposed to ride the Broom-Go-Round after we get a shadow twist."

Wiggling a finger in my ear, I shook my head. "What now? Shadow twist? Broom-Go-Round?"

Trina laughed. "Sorry, I forget sometimes you're not used to all this stuff. A shadow twist is this chocolate pastry with fairy powder all over the top. It's so good, I could eat a billion of them." She opened her arms wide in the air, a fierce expression on her face.

"It sounds like it." I covered my mouth and giggled. "What about a Broom-Go-Round? Can I assume it's what it sounds like?"

"Well, kind of. They have single and tandem brooms you can ride with your date. The brooms are spelled to go around in a circle and, well ..." She sighed. "You'll just have to see it for yourself."

"I'll put it on my list."

She crossed her arms, her shoulders coming up by her ears. "You know, it's really too bad you are stuck at your booth all night. This would be a great place for you to have a date with your guys. In any case, I'm going to go shower and find Libby. See you in a few."

I waved and then went about setting up my pamphlets. My stomach growled, reminding me I'd only had a muffin this morning as I worked through lunch. I glanced at my booth and then over at Sabrina who was texting, not even paying attention to me. It should be safe for me to go grab something to eat.

Stephanie was loitering near the section we'd set up the booth, texting away on her phone. She was pretty reliable, so I bet I could get her to watch my booth.

"Hey, Steph," I called out to her.

She glanced up from her phone and headed my way. "Max, what's up?" She glanced at my booth and gestured to it. "Cool booth."

"Thanks." I beamed with pride. "Do you have a minute? I wanted to go grab something to eat but don't want to leave my booth unattended."

"Oh, sure." Steph nodded. "I'd be happy to watch it. Just bring me back a soda, huh?"

"Sure," I grinned. "I'll be back in a few."

As Steph took a seat behind the booth, I sat my notecards underneath the counter. I waved at her and then headed toward the cafeteria.

I was surprised to find out that the Spring Fair wasn't just for the contest. All kinds of students set up booths at the fair. The charm club made several rides for people to ride, one of those being the Broom-Go-Round that Trina was so excited to go on with Libby. There were also a lot of food stands that smelled like they were going to be absolutely delicious. Sadly, they weren't open yet, and I was forced to eat cafeteria food.

I pushed past the students starting to gather in the courtyard and made my way inside. Even with the students waiting for the fair to start, there was still a long line in the cafeteria.

Sighing, I took my place in line, my foot tapping with impatience. I didn't want to stay away from my booth for too long just in case someone came by wanting more information, or worse if the judges came by early. I didn't put it past Sabrina to try and mess with me to make herself look better, but I hoped there were enough people around to keep her from getting too bold.

"Hey." An arm slid around my waist, and my senses were filled with Ian's dark chocolate and musk.

Sinking into his embrace, I leaned my head back to look up at him. "What are you doing here? I thought you were helping with the dark arts exhibit?"

Ian bent down and captured my lips with his, earning a bunch of swoon-worthy points from every girl around us and me. When he released my lips, my knees threatened to come out from beneath me, and the line had moved several feet ahead of us.

"We finished setting up already. I figured I'd grab something to eat before the crowds start pouring in."

"Great minds think alike."

A throat cleared behind us, and I released Ian long enough to see the glares being shot our way from the line behind us. Flushing, I hurried the few feet forward with Ian beside me, smirking like I was the funniest thing he'd ever seen.

I grabbed a tray from the pile and side-eyed him. "What?"

"Nothing." Ian sat his tray next to mine, bumping it down the line. "I just find it funny how easily you're embarrassed."

"I'm not embarrassed."

"Your red cheeks would say otherwise."

Immediately, my hands went to my cheeks, and I scowled as he chuckled. I picked a French fry off the plate I'd just placed on my tray and tossed it at him. He cocked a brow at me in return. "Yeah, I did that."

We moved further down the line, and as I was reaching for an orange, a ghostly hand squeezed my breast. I gasped and dropped the orange. I shot Ian a look, but he was intently studying the tuna salad like it might tell his future. Not convinced but not wanting to get yelled at by the rest of the line, I turned back the orange. This time, when I grabbed the orange, the ghost hand squeezed my ass.

Jumping in place, I turned to Ian who had a slight grin on his lips. "Would you stop that?"

"Stop what?" he asked innocently, taking a bite of an apple before pushing our trays down the line.

Frowning at him but not believing he wasn't the owner of the ghost hand, I continued to fill my tray with food. Every once in a while, the ghost hand would reappear for no reason other than to drive me crazy. A squeeze here, a slip of the hand there. By the time I got to the cashier, I was a horny ball of tension.

"Five fifty," the cashier told me.

I dug into my pocket to pull out my money, and a ghost finger rubbed the top of my core. A small, strangled noise slipped out of my mouth, causing the cashier to give me a worried frown. "Sorry, just really hungry." I handed her the money and hurried away with a chuckling Ian close behind me.

"That was not funny," I growled at Ian as he took the seat next to me.

"I thought it was," Ian quipped, lifting his sandwich up to his mouth. I let my irritation and magic billow up inside of me, and the sandwich jerked to the left, smearing tuna onto his cheek. Eyes narrowed, Ian tried again. This time, it moved up and slapped him in the nose.

When he lowered the sandwich, I stifled a laugh. Some of the tuna had ended up in his nose. I turned my head and stuffed my mouth with a French fry before Ian could see me looking.

"You're going to pay for that." Ian dropped his sandwich on his plate, using his napkin to clean his hands before reaching for me.

I tensed for his attack, but Monica came rushing up to our table. "Max! Come quick."

Wiping my hands off, I stood up to meet Monica. "What is it? What's wrong?"

"It's your booth." She winced like she didn't want to be the one to tell me. Monica's leg jiggled, and her hands twisted in front of her.

“What about my booth?” I said slowly, my heart beginning to race in fear of what Monica might say.

She clenched her teeth and made a sort of whining noise before dropping her hands. “I think you better just come see. It’s not good.”

Frown deepening, I glanced toward Ian who stood from the table. We rushed from the cafeteria and out into the courtyard. A crowd had begun to gather around the area my booth was in, not making me feel any better about what could have happened.

I shoved my way through the crowd, Ian close on my heels. I could barely hear any of the voices over the sound of my own heart, and none of them were kind. When I finally got through the crowd and saw my booth, my heart stopped in my chest.

“I’m so sorry, Max. I only moved away for a minute, I swear.” Stephanie cried, her eyes full of unshed tears. She twisted her hair in her hand like she might pull it out at the root.

“It’s okay, Steph. It’s not your fault.” I tried to reassure the girl even though my insides twisted into a knot.

“What the fuck?” Ian muttered next to me, his hand taking mine in his.

The booth that Trina and I had slaved over all morning and most of the afternoon had been turned into a horror show. Large holes were busted in the side of the booth as well as the roof. The pale blue paint had been plastered over with red paint spelling 'Mancaster Whore.'

My mouth dropped open, completely astounded by the amount of damage done in such a small amount of time and in full view of so many witnesses. Scanning the crowd, my eyes landed on Sabrina snickering by herself as she watched from her booth.

Anger burned in my veins, my magic crackling along my skin. Stomping across the courtyard, I didn't even need to push the people aside, they just moved on their own. The voices quieted as I stopped before Sabrina who barely looked up from her phone to greet me.

"Oh, Norman. It's you." She dryly droned and then smirked. "Too bad about your booth. I heard you had quite the controversial topic to present. I bet you could have even won first place."

Propping my fists on my hips, I snarled, "And you wouldn't know anything about who did this would you?"

"Who, me?" Sabrina stood from her seat and brushed her hair over her shoulder as if I were asking her the time of day. "Not that you care, but I don't need to break your booth to beat you. I'll beat you with my status, flair, and ..." She eyed me up and down with a sniff. "Well let's just face it. I'm far classier than you."

I snorted. "Sure, you are."

Sabrina rolled her eyes and sat back down, pulling her phone out and typing away. Of course, Sabrina would believe that. It still left the mystery of who would destroy my booth.

Turning my attention back to my booth, I groaned. How was I going to fix all this before the fair started? It had taken me all morning to make it, and that was with Trina's help.

When I returned to my booth, I found the crowd had been scared away by the appearance of Aidan. He loomed over the area, his silent brooding dissuading anybody from coming to gossip or take pictures. Behind him, Ian, Paul, and Dale had their heads bowed close together as they whispered amongst themselves.

"Hey, guys." I tucked my hands in my pockets and watched as they jumped in place and spun around like they had been caught doing something they shouldn't have. "What's going on?"

"Nothing," Dale said a bit too quickly, pushing his glasses up with his finger. The other two nodded their heads in agreement, but I wasn't buying it. Settling them with my best cough it up glower, I watched with growing amusement as they began to shift and fidget.

"Fine. You got us." Paul grinned, his hands up in the air. "We were discussing who could have had it out for you and the best spell to fix your booth."

"A spell? What spell?"

"The time reversal spell." Ian adjusted his stance, crossing his arms over his chest. "It allows the caster to reverse time to a certain point on a single object."

My mouth dropped open slightly. "I knew you could stop time, but you can really reverse it?"

"Of course." Dale grinned, puffing his chest up with pride. "But the amount of time you are able to go back depends on the strength of the person casting it. Since this had to have happened while you and Ian were in the cafeteria, it couldn't have been more than twenty minutes. Child's play."

"That's great." I clasped my hands in front of me, tempted to jump up and down in excitement. "I don't know what I would do without you guys." I allowed myself to approach each of them, kissing them on the cheek in turn. Ian, of course, couldn't keep his hands to himself and snuck a squeeze of my ass causing me to giggle.

"Alright, then." I clapped my hands together. "Let's get this done and quickly."

"Aight, madam." Dale mock saluted me and turned to the booth.

“Hold up,” I grabbed his shoulder stopping him. “I want to do it. It’s my booth. It only makes sense for me to fix it.”

Dale studied me for a moment and then nodded. “Alright. You’re up.”

“So, what do I do?” I asked, taking a step toward the booth.

Coming up beside me, Dale murmured into my ear. “Take a deep breath and lift your hands.” Even though I felt a bit silly, I did as he asked and brought my hands up in front of me. “Now, focus. Think about what your booth looked like before. You need your magic to pinpoint the exact moment you last saw it, so it can use it as a guiding point for where it’s going.”

I brought the image of the booth into my mind’s eye, thinking of how I’d left my booth before. The pale blue wood Trina and I had spent all morning laboring over. At first, nothing happened. I thought maybe I was doing it wrong but then the air began to thicken, and the hair on my arms stood on end. The booth shifted and then, like I was watching a video going in reverse, the booth changed. The slanderous graffiti disappeared one letter at a time, and the holes in the wood filled back in. When I was done, I was disappointed to find that my pamphlets still laid all over the floor.

"There! Good as new. Or almost." Dale grimaced at the mess on the ground. Before I even asked, he cast another spell making the pamphlets float off the ground and pile themselves back on the table I'd set up. "There. Now, it's good as new."

"Thanks, Dale." I squeezed his arm and sighed. "I just wish I knew who had done it."

Chapter 23

MAYBE I COULD USE my amulet to just win the competition. I had two wishes left, and technically it was within the rules of amulet's powers. I wasn't creating anything or killing anyone.

But it would be cheating.

Only if you get caught.

Really? That's what we were going with? I'm not Sabrina. I didn't do crap like that. I had never cheated in my life. I was not going to start now.

So I said to myself. However, despite my noble intentions, it didn't take away from the fact that I was in big trouble. The fair had begun, and I'd had barely any people come to my booth, and when I say barely, I mean, like, two. That was not going to win me any scholarships.

I sighed heavily, my gaze scanning the crowd hanging out at Sabrina's booth. She might be an elitist bitch, but it was working for her. All I had was four hot wizards doing their best to show their support. Well, sort of.

Dale and Paul were talking about the differences between the use of poppy seeds and the actual poppy in home-brewed potions. It would have been a quite invigorating debate had it not been on such a boring topic. Ian had his legs propped up on the edge of my booth, leaning back in the chair he had conjured out of thin air and looking very much like the sexy bad boy. And then there was Aiden. Sweet, big as a mountain Aiden. If anyone were deterring my audience, it would be him. While I found him adorable in his stalkerish ways, the quiet looming would make any man or woman quake in their boots.

"Hey, honey," my mom strolled up, holding hands with my dad. "Your booth is nice."

"It sucks, mom." I sighed and stood. "I can't get anyone to come over here."

My dad's eyes weren't on me and the booth but the guys hanging around it. "Well, it's probably because you have your own set of bodyguards here. Maybe lose some of the testosterone."

I gave my dad a wry grin. "Thanks, dad, I'll keep that in mind."

"So, when do the judges come by?" my mom asked. She was trying to hide her anxiety, I could tell. She was rubbing my dad's arm like it was a magic lamp. If something did pop out of my dad, I sure as hell hoped I wasn't there for it.

I shrugged. "Probably pretty soon, but if I don't get some more people, it won't matter."

"Well, then." Mom glanced around at the guys. "We better get you some more people. You." She pointed at Ian. "Go find some girls, throw a little flirty smile their way, and then lead them over here."

"Why him?" Dale asked, clearly miffed by my mom's choice.

She raised her brows. "Look at him. He's got that bad boy thing down pat. No girl can resist a bad boy."

"Mom," I warned. The last thing I needed was for her to be showing favoritism. I had enough pissing contests between them on my own. She didn't need to start something where there wasn't anything.

"I'm just saying." She gestured to Dale. "You have a lot going for you too, but we aren't at a library. We're at a festival where girls are going to be looking for the fun guy, not the 'I'll let you in my pants if you help me with my homework' guy."

"Peggy!" my dad admonished.

She laughed and patted his chest. "Don't worry, dear. You can still teach me anytime you want."

"Mom, ew."

"Quite right. That is hardly an appropriate conversation to be having in public or other." My grandmother pushed her way into our little group. "Maxine," she nodded at me and then to each of the guys in turn, except for Dale. She stared hard at him and then turned her back, clearly telling everyone what she thought of him.

Dale didn't appear to notice, or he was hiding it. I had a feeling I was going to have to deal with it later regardless of the fact. Just what I needed.

"Grandmother, how nice to see you." I gave her an awkward hug and glanced behind her. "Where's grandfather?"

"Oh, he's about." She waved a hand behind her. "He loves these kinds of things, especially shadow twists." A soft smile caused her lips to curl. She seemed to catch herself, and she smoothed out her face a stern frown taking its place as she turned to my mom. "I'm surprised you took time out of your busy life of playing in the dirt to come support your daughter."

"Mother," my mom snapped, stepping between her and my dad.

"No, it's alright, Peggy." My dad pushed her behind him and stood in front of my grandmother. My grandmother's eyes bore into him as if daring him to say something.

"This is a bunch of bull crap." I sighed, scratching my face with my hand. "I can't deal with this right now guys. I have a contest to win. I can't referee a pissing match between you too."

"Maxine!"

"Max!"

Grabbing my amulet, I didn't even hesitate. "I wish everyone could get along until the end of the competition."

All of a sudden, the irritation and resentment on my parents and grandmother's face melted away. A sort of artificial calm replaced it, and they all smiled at each other.

Turning away from them, I gestured to Ian. "Can you go do what my mom suggested? It'd really help."

"Of course," Ian smirked, sauntering over to me. He leaned down and pressed his lips to mine with a wink. "Anything for you." I watched him walk away a little too long because Paul cleared his throat.

"Yeah, sorry. Uh, Dale and Paul, can you start handing out the pamphlets? Get as many people as you can to come this way?" The guys nodded and then I turned to Aidan. "Aidan, you're really awesome as a bodyguard, but in this instance, I think—"

"Say no more." Aidan nodded and moved from my booth to stand beside Sabrina's. Instantly, the people around her booth started to get nervous. Many of them quickly leaving and heading my way.

Clapping my hands with a gleeful grin, my faith was renewed. I glanced at my family and waved them away. "Go enjoy the fair, I've got a contest to win." To the crowd coming toward me, I gave them my best professional smile. "The future of the magical community is here. Come and find out how you can help keep balance in our lives."

By the time the judges came around, I'd run out of pamphlets and had so many people at my booth they had to push their way through. I was surprised by the reaction I'd gotten from many of the visitors. Most of them didn't even realize there was an issue, and the others thought it was a great idea. I only had a few who balked at my suggestions.

"I'm not human-raised, why should I care?"

"Yes," the headmaster who was one of the judges agreed. "Why should we care?"

Clearing my throat, my hands becoming moist. I held them behind my back to hide how they shook and to keep myself from fidgeting. "I'm glad you asked. While the percentage of human-raised witches and wizards is one in nine, leaving them to fend for themselves would be detrimental to our community as a whole. Would you really want to let a bunch of children barely old enough to vote figuring out the confines of their powers? Can you imagine the chaos that could create?

"I am human-raised and can tell you that it scared me. My powers came out when my emotions became too much to hold onto. So, they manifested through my power and almost killed several people."

"Then we should just get rid of them then," someone in the crowd called out. A few people agreed with them.

"How are you going to find them?" I asked, glancing around the group. "Are you going to hunt them down in the trillions of people in the world? You might as well be searching for a snowflake in a snowstorm.

"The fact is we need new regulations for those who were human-raised, something other than just throwing them into school and hoping they catch up. Because, believe me, it's not fun. We are taking away the chance to have some amazing witches and wizards by handicapping them for something they had no control over."

"And what do you propose?" another judge asked, this one a brunette woman with glasses that pointed up at the ends.

Taking a deep breath, I took one of my flyers and showed it to her. "I propose a spell that would only be available to those who are human-raised, one that would fill in the years of education that we missed, just like that. Then we are caught up and are no longer a danger to society."

"But if we do it for you, why shouldn't we do it for all magical children?" the headmaster asked. There was a proud sort of look on his face that gave me the courage to continue.

"I don't think they would want it, to be honest. I know I wouldn't. I'd rather have the experience of going through school, finding new friends, and making my own mistakes over having twelve years' worth of schooling shoved into my head. However, since that is not an option, there would have to be regulations that stated the spell would only be available to those who need it. Meaning only a set amount of people would know the spell, and they would be kept to secrecy by a binding spell, limiting those who would abuse the system to a minimum."

The crowd around me clapped politely. The judges had pleased expressions, or at least they looked so, as they scribbled away on their pads of paper. They moved on to the other booths, allowing me to finally relax.

Dale came up behind me, placing a hand on my shoulder. "You did great."

"Really?"

"Yes." He nodded, pulling me close. "I couldn't have said it better myself."

"He is right." Aidan approached.

I grabbed onto his arm, hugging him tightly. "So, can you tell me? Who won?"

Aidan's lip twitched. "No."

"Ah, come on." I stomped my foot and pouted. Aidan bent down and thumbed my lower lip before brushing his against mine. I placed my hand on the side of his face and leaned into him. When he released me, I sighed. "Fine. I'll wait."

Chapter 24

WAITING FOR THE ANNOUNCEMENT was torture. They weren't kind enough to make a decision right away. They had to brood over it for an hour or two. It was enough to make a girl sprout some gray hairs!

"Relax." Paul smoothed a hand over my back. "It'll be all over soon. I'm sure you'll do fine."

I nodded but still chewed on my thumbnail. He might be able to keep calm because he had his family money to take care of his schooling. If I let my grandmother pay for it, she'd own me, and I wasn't ready to give up my freedom just yet.

Dale sat at my other side, his hand on my leg. "If you don't win, you can always do a work-study like me. There's a few available in the library."

I grimaced. I knew Dale was being helpful, but I really didn't want to have to work and do school at the same time, not if I could help it. I had a hard enough time keeping up with my work as it was. If I had to work too, I couldn't imagine the amount of stress that would add to my plate.

"Thanks, I'll keep that in mind." I'd put that in my list of last resorts, along with student loans and stripping.

"Hello, can I have your attention please?" a voice boomed over the entire fairgrounds.

I couldn't see the speaker even though I knew where it was coming from. I got out of my seat and started toward the stage they'd set up. The guys followed after me, each of them staying close by my side. My parents and grandparents had done exactly as my wish had commanded. They chatted happily with each other as if they were best friends. It was a bit eerie actually.

Turning my attention from them, I focused my gaze on the stage. The headmaster stood with the other judges waiting for everyone to quieten.

"Thank you all for coming out. We appreciate your support in the school and our students. Now the moment everyone has been waiting for ..."

My heart jumped into my throat, and my pulse pounded in my ears. This was the moment that would decide the fate of my future. Okay, that was a bit dramatic, but it was still a really big deal. Student loans were no joke.

"We are proud to announce that the winner of this year's Spring Fair competition, by a unanimous vote, is Maxine Mancaster!"

The crowd cheered, and the guys patted me on the back. My mom hugged me, and my grandparents gave me congratulations. All of this was barely registered in my shocked system.

I couldn't believe it, I had won. I had really won. It took me several seconds to process what was happening and then it hit me. What the headmaster had called me.

Mancaster. He'd called me Maxine Mancaster, not Norman.

Fury and disappointment filled me. I had won alright.

People had liked my idea, sure, but my booth wasn't really all that, and I wasn't that charming. The reason I had won wasn't that I'd had a great idea. Or I'd charmed the judges. It was because I was a Mancaster.

Without a word, I pushed away from the hands on me and through the crowd. I had to talk to the headmaster. I couldn't accept it. I wouldn't. I had said from the beginning that I'd make my way with my parent's name. My name. I wasn't some magical royalty that got things handed to them.

However, I never got to the headmaster. Someone rushed up to the stage and whispered in his ear. His face went from happy to despair in under a millisecond. He didn't explain but moved off the stage and out of sight.

I stood there in all my anger and confusion, not knowing what to do. My grandmother came up to my side, her hand on my shoulder. The look on her face told me she knew what was wrong.

"What is it?" I glanced back at my grandmother and the sympathy on her face genuine.

"It's his daughter, Delilah. She's dying."

"Dying?" My brow scrunched together, trying to remember when they had mentioned her before. My grandmother had offered her condolences before, but they had never said what was wrong with her. "Of what?"

"Cancer."

"Don't you have some kind of spell for that?" I asked, not understanding how that was even a thing for them.

My grandmother gave me a small, sad smile. "Magic can do many things, but even it cannot fight death."

I frowned hard at her answer. My amulet warmed against my chest as if telling me I could do something. I glanced down at my amulet, the inside of the gem swirling and sparkling like never before. I never would have thought to use it, not for this. Surely, it wasn't powerful enough to save someone's life. It couldn't even make money.

But I had to try.

"I have to go," I told my grandmother, heading toward the way the headmaster went. I could hear them calling my name behind me, but I didn't stop. I ended up at the entrance to the fair, but I had no idea where to go from there. I didn't even know where the headmaster had gone.

A rumbling noise came toward me, and I jumped back as Ian came to a stop in front of me, a motorcycle growling beneath his legs. "Get on."

Not one to be told twice, I hopped on the back of the bike. "Do you know where you're going?"

"The headmaster's house, right?" I nodded. He revved the engine. "Then hold on."

We raced down the street faster than I'd ever gone. I wasn't even sure he was going the speed limit, but none of the cars even noticed we were going by them. Deciding he had to have some kind of spell at work, I held onto him like my life depended on it.

Before I knew it, we were at the headmaster's home. I expected his house to be like my grandparents' or the Broomsteins', but it was a simple home like my parents', a two-story house with off grey paneling. There were several cars parked outside, and a feeling of gloom had settled over the place.

I climbed off Ian's bike and started toward the house. Ian trailed after me. I didn't really acknowledge him as I walked up the steps and rang the doorbell. At first, no one answered, and I thought I might have to ring it again, but then there was a rush of feet and the door opened. The headmaster stood there, grief and confusion on his face.

"Miss Norman, Mr. Broomstein, I'm not sure what you are doing here but now is not a good time. I will see you at school." He tried to shut the door on us, but I caught it.

"Wait, please. I want to help." I licked my lips as he stared at me. "I mean, I think I can. If you'll let me."

He seemed to struggle with his decision. Not surprising, really. However, when he moved back and allowed us inside, I sighed with relief.

"I'm not sure what you think you can do, but she's this way." He led us through his home in a slow gait. It was humbly decorated, nothing like the other wizard homes I'd visited, not that they were the norm.

We came to a bedroom door on the first floor. The door was half cracked, and I could hear low voices inside. The headmaster pushed the door open and went in.

I hesitated.

Ian took my hand, squeezing it lightly. My hand around the amulet, I stepped into the room.

Headmaster Swordson took his place by the bed, next to what I could only assume was his wife. A few others hovered nearby, all of them looking at me like they couldn't understand what I was doing there. A weak cough came from the bed.

Delilah could have been called beautiful at one point but no longer. Her hair was drab, her face shallow, and almost skeletal. Cancer had wrung her out and left her to dry. It was clear in her eyes that she knew death was coming and she accepted it.

But I didn't. I could do something for them, for this family that I didn't know but whose father had already made a huge impact on my life.

"Hello," I said quietly to the room. "I'm Max. This is Ian." I gestured to him. They all nodded politely but didn't greet us. I turned to the headmaster. "Can I?"

"Of course." He moved away from the bed, allowing me to take a seat beside Delilah.

"Hi, Delilah, how are you?" I snorted. "Sorry, that's a stupid question."

The woman smiled weakly.

"I don't know if this will work, but I'm going to try and help you. I just need you to relax is all. Can you do that?" Delilah's hand twitched.

"Right, not like you have a choice." To the headmaster, I asked, "Where's the cancer?"

"In her liver but it's spread to her blood and other organs," the headmaster offered.

"So pretty much everywhere. Alright," I fingered my amulet, "I guess that makes it easier then." My eyes went to Ian who gave me an encouraging thumbs up, the douche.

I placed my hand on Delilah's. I wasn't sure if I needed to be touching her, but it couldn't hurt. My other hand stayed on the amulet, and I could feel it begin to warm as my wish formulated in my mind. "I wish the cancer was gone."

"What is this crap?" an annoyed voice from the grievers asked but he was shushed by everyone else.

"I wish she was healthy. I wish the cancer were gone." I kept muttering these wishes over and over again, but the amulet never grew to that almost hot temperature like it had with all my other wishes.

Maybe it was too big for it? Dad had bought it at a marketplace in Cairo. It's not like it was a lifesaving object.

Just as I was about to give up, the ball of light in my mind's eye flared at me. I cocked my head to the side as if trying to listen to it. It was trying to tell me something just like the amulet had.

Suddenly, I knew what to do.

My hand still on the amulet, I reached out with my mind and grasped a hold of my magic, coaxing it to move through me and into the stone. If it didn't have enough power to grant my wish, then I'd have to lend it some of mine. I fed it my magic until the amulet grew so warm that it stung my hand, but I didn't let it go.

Power pulsated in my hand, waiting for me to give it a direction. My other hand still sat on Delilah's leathery skin, so it was easy enough to redirect the magic through me and into her. My eyes were screwed tightly shut, concentrating on giving her the magic and pushing all my intentions into it. I couldn't see if it was working or not.

Someone gasped, but I didn't stop. I kept pushing the magic into her until I felt lightheaded myself. The hand beneath mine stirred and then turned over to clasp mine, tightly.

"Max," a voice said in my ear, but it sounded so far off. "You can stop now, Max."

I couldn't bring myself to answer or to stop. It was like I had opened a hole in myself and I couldn't plug it back up. I could feel every piece of myself leaking away, making me weaker and tired.

"Max, you have to let go." Those were the last words I heard before everything went black.

Chapter 25

MY HEAD HURT, AND my mouth felt like I'd been rolling a cotton ball around in it. I groaned and shifted in bed.

Wait, bed? I blinked my eyes opened and then immediately shut them. Too bright. Way too bright.

"Miss Norman," the headmaster's voice came from my left side.

"Am I dead?" I asked, hissing as I tried to sit up. My body ached all over, and I gave up trying to get up.

"No, you are very much alive as is my daughter, thanks to you."

My eyes shot open, and I blinked against the light to look at him. "Delilah's alive? I did it?"

Headmaster Swordson inclined his head. "She is."

When he told me I had won the competition, I had a hard time believing him. Now with him in front of me telling me I had saved his daughter's life, I didn't doubt him for a second. But still, it was remarkable.

"I'm happy I could help." A thought came to mind, and before I could lose my nerve, I asked, "About the contest. I only won because of my grandparents, didn't I?"

Folding his hands in front of him, the headmaster cleared his throat. "It is unfortunate to say your parentage did get brought up during the deliberations. However, your heritage was actually a point against you. It was only by your inspiring speech that you were able to claim your victory."

"Really?" I squeaked in surprise.

"Yes, it might behoove you to know that not everyone adores the elite like our Miss Craftsman may have you believe. There are several, who in fact, envy and despise those like you who have all the wealth and influence and would love to see you fail." He took a deep breath and then continued, "However, even if it hadn't been the case, your actions today. Putting a complete stranger's well being above your own? You showed great strength of character. You are more than worthy of the scholarship."

I nodded, still not quite happy about winning.

Headmaster Swordson shifted before me. "Several people are waiting to see you. I should let them come in."

"Yeah, sure. I'm sure my mom is just freaking out."

"And many others." He smiled.

"By the way," I asked, glancing around the room that was not mine. "Where am I?"

Turning the doorknob, he answered, "The infirmary, Miss Norman."

Before he completely left, several people pushed past him into the room. The first person to approach me had no qualms about jumping on the bed with a squeal.

"Oh, my god, Max!" Trina screamed, hugging me tightly. "Don't do that to me! I thought you died."

"Love you too, Trina." I winced, patting her on the back. "Can't breathe."

"Oh, sorry." She released me promptly and jumped off the bed, allowing my guys to come into my line of vision.

"Hey," Ian smiled, kneeling by the bed. "There's my girl. You scared me there for a minute." He brushed my hair away from my face, his fingers lingering on my cheek.

"Sorry," I placed my hand on top of his, leaning into his touch. "I didn't realize it would take so much out of me."

"That's because of the amount of magic you used." Dale pushed his glasses up his nose, leaning against the end of the bed. "Many practitioners have suffered from overuse. You'll regain your abilities in a few days."

It was then that I realized the ball of light in my head was more like a dim flicker. Huh. Guess I was completely tapped out.

"It's remarkable what you did." Paul sat down on the bed next to me. "I'm sure the headmaster is grateful."

"More than grateful," Aidan added in, seeming a bit put off by the whole thing. Was he mad? I tried to meet his eyes, but he looked away.

"Don't mind him, he's been pissy all day." Ian waved Aidan off. "Big guy doesn't do helpless well."

"Aw, I'm sorry. I really didn't mean to make you worry." My eyes burned with emotion, not knowing what to do to make him feel better.

"Alright guys!" Trina clapped her hands together. "We saw her, she's alive. Now I think she needs some rest."

My stomach growled loudly.

Trina giggled and winked. "And maybe some food. Let's go. Out." She whipped her hand in the air, ordering the guys around quite easily.

Ian kissed me, followed by his brother, and then Dale, leaving with Trina. Aidan hovered behind, and I held my hand out to him.

"I didn't see," he said softly, pain in his face.

"It's okay, big guy, you can't see everything." I kissed the back of his hand, pressing it to my face. "Thank you for being here."

Nodding but not saying anything more, Aidan gave my hand a squeeze before heading for the door.

The next person that came in thankfully was my mom. I sat up in bed as she came in her arms open wide to hug me. She gathered me up in her arms, pressing me tightly to her. I inhaled deeply, breathing her in.

"How are you feeling, honey?" she pulled back and smoothed my hair away from my face.

"Surprisingly sore and starving."

"Well, let me get you something." She started to stand, but I stopped her.

"The guys are already on it." I chuckled. "In fact, they are probably bringing enough food for an army so stick around. You can help me eat it."

Laughing, my mom shifted next to me. "I'm glad you have found someone to care for you here, even if it's several someones. You need some happiness in your life."

"I have that already."

"You know what I mean." She smiled softly.

"Yeah, I do. They're great though." I mused, my heart warming as I thought about them.

"Well, it has to be hard."

"What?"

"Juggling four guys."

I snorted. "Not really." She gave me a pointed look. "Okay, so it's a bit complicated.

A lot of refereeing. Hurt feelings and such. Don't even get me started on figuring out where all the penises go. It's just—"

"Okay, okay. I get it. You can stop."

Laughing at her horrified expression, I stopped. Didn't want to give my mom a heart attack twice in one day. Regardless of my near-death experience, I'd secured my magical future – at least for next year – and had gotten even closer to the guys. I couldn't have asked for a better end to my first year at Winchester Academy. Plus, I saved someone's life. What could be better than that?

Thank You for Reading!

Want to find out what happens to Max next?

Follow me on social media to be one of the first to find out!

Don't want to interact but want to be on the up and up?

Follow me on Social Media

Facebook.com/erinrbedford

@erin_bedford

Want to be the first to know about my new releases?

erinbedford.com/newsletter

Made in the USA
Las Vegas, NV
05 September 2024